mary-kate olsen ashley olsen

so little time

Check out these other great

so little time

titles:

Book 1: **how to train a boy**

Book 2: **instant boyfriend**

Book 3: **too good to be true**

Book 4: **just between us**

Book 5: **tell me about it**

Book 6: **secret crush**

Book 7: **girl talk**

Coming soon!

Book 9: **dating game**

mary-kate olsen **ashley** olsen

so little **time**

the love factor

Written by Rosalind Noonan

Based on the teleplay by Becky Southwell

HarperEntertainment
An Imprint of HarperCollins*Publishers*

A PARACHUTE PRESS BOOK

A PARACHUTE PRESS BOOK

Parachute Publishing, L.L.C.
156 Fifth Avenue, Suite 302
New York, NY 10010

Published by
HarperEntertainment
An Imprint of HarperCollins*Publishers*
10 East 53rd Street, New York, NY 10022-5299

ISBN 0-06-009312-9

First printing: March 2003

Printed in the United States of America

Visit HarperEntertainment on the World Wide Web at
www.harpercollins.com

10 9 8 7 6 5 4 3 2 1

chapter one

"Chloe, are we here for a reason?" fourteen-year-old Riley Carlson asked her twin sister. "Or is this one of those unsolved mysteries?"

Chloe, Riley, and their friend Sierra Pomeroy were sitting at a table at a coffee bar called the Newsstand. Chloe only half heard her sister's question. She was busy watching Lennon Porter make coffee behind the counter. She was drawn to him—but why? Was it his crooked smile? Or the way his curly dark hair fell over his eyes...?

"Earth to Chloe?" Sierra pinged her shoulder. "Come back, girl!"

Chloe tore her eyes away from Lennon. She wasn't ready to admit that she came to the Newsstand just to stare at him. She didn't like him at all—she really didn't! He was such a know-it-all, but so cute.... So she tried to think of a non-Lennon reason for dragging Riley and Sierra to the café.

"Isn't this place cool?" she said lamely. "Look at all the magazines! They have lots of PCs and newspapers. And good scenery."

"Yeah, we're here for the scenery, all right," Riley said, turning toward the counter.

Lennon reached up and placed two glasses on a high shelf.

"Why don't you just admit it, Chloe?" Riley continued. "You like Lennon!"

"What are you talking about?" Chloe said. "I can't stand him." Chloe glanced over at him, then turned away. "Don't stare! You guys are so obvious!"

"Come on, Chloe. Come clean," Sierra said. "You're totally crushing on him."

"Crushing?" Chloe felt her cheeks heat up. "That is so not true. Lennon is an obnoxious jerk. He's so full of himself! How could you even think I like him?"

"Because it's true?" Riley asked with a grin.

Chloe rolled her eyes. She hated it when her sister was right. "Fine—he's cute, okay? Look at the guy! No—don't!"

Riley and Sierra had turned to glance at Lennon again. They jerked their heads back toward Chloe, giggling.

"You can't hide it, Chloe," Sierra teased. "You totally like him."

"That's impossible," Chloe protested. "He thinks he knows everything, and I hate people like that." The trouble was, Lennon really *did* seem to know everything. Or a lot, at least.

The waitress came by, and the three girls ordered coffee drinks.

Riley leaned toward Chloe, her shoulder-length blond hair brushing the tabletop. "Maybe Lennon will bus our table when we're done. That'll give you a chance to talk to him."

Chloe sniffed. "I have nothing to say to the guy."

"That's a lie, and you know it," Sierra said. "You're *dying* to ask him out!"

"Talk to us, Chloe," Riley said. "We'll help you. I got Sierra and Larry together, and look how great that's turning out."

Sierra had started going out with Larry Slotnick, who was sweet but kind of goofy. Make that *way* goofy. But Sierra seemed to really like him. She thought he had a great sense of humor, and that he wasn't afraid to be himself.

"Okay, you're right," Chloe admitted. "I've been trying to think of a way to ask out Lennon. But how? He's not like other guys. He's traveled all over the world and speaks twenty-five zillion languages."

"So?" Riley said. "There's nothing wrong with that."

"But he's so stuck up about it," Chloe went on. "He thinks he's perfect. And he can be so rude—and stubborn!"

She'd met Lennon when they both volunteered at a senior citizens' center, and she had problems with him from the beginning. How could she even think of asking him out?

"You know what?" Chloe said. "This was a bad idea. Let's get out of here." She grabbed her bag.

"We can't. Alex and Larry are meeting us here," Riley reminded her. Alex Zimmer was Riley's boyfriend.

"And we already ordered frappes," Sierra added. "Stay and face your fears!" she whispered in a spooky voice.

"I'm not afraid of him," Chloe insisted. "I'm just not sure how I feel about him. I'm all confused." She plopped back down and watched Lennon carry a bin of dirty dishes into the kitchen. His apron was slung low over his hips. His hair was a little longer than most guys' and curled over his collar. Lennon had a style of his own.

He came out of the kitchen and hurried over to a Japanese couple who were leaving. "*Domo arrigato*!" Lennon said, bowing.

The Japanese man and woman bowed, too. Smiling, they chatted with Lennon in Japanese. And he schmoozed right back.

"What a show-off," Chloe said. "Do you see? That is why I can't go out with him."

"I think it's sweet," Sierra said.

Riley rolled her eyes. "Chloe's right. The guy's totally showing off."

The Japanese couple left, and Lennon returned to the counter. Chloe looked around for something to distract her from him. She reached for a copy of her favorite magazine, *Teen Style*. "Hey, there's a quiz in this month's issue!" She flipped to the table of contents. "Let's take it right now."

"I already had a pop quiz in Spanish today," Riley complained. "Isn't one enough?"

"This is a really good one," Chloe promised. "It's called 'The Love Factor: Is Your Boyfriend the Right Boy for You?'"

"I'll take it," Sierra offered. "Though it might not work for me. I mean, we're talking about Larry."

"It's true." Riley nodded. "Larry is definitely in a category of his own."

[Chloe: Larry used to be crazy about Riley—before he fell for Sierra. But when I say crazy, I mean crazy! He bounced up to her bedroom window on a trampoline. He collected all her used yogurt containers and built sand castles for her. I guess you have to give him points for creativity.]

"'The Love Factor quiz is foolproof!'" Chloe read from the magazine.

Sierra shrugged. "Right, but is it Larry-proof?"

Chloe licked her lips. "We'll see about that. But I'll just have to keep score since I don't have a boyfriend. At least, not at the moment."

"Why don't you take it with Lennon in mind?" Riley asked.

"Please! Let's not even go there." Chloe clicked her pen and prepared to write. "Okay, question number one," she said. "'Your love gives you a gift wrapped with a big fat bow. You're thrilled...until you open it. It's all wrong for you! You... A. throw it in his face, B. tell him you'll cherish it forever because it's from him, C. admit it's not your style though you appreciate the thought, or D. take it home and sew it into a quilt.'"

"Who are they kidding?" Riley said. "All the choices are ridiculous."

"B," Sierra said firmly. When Riley and Chloe stared at her, she shrugged. "I guess I'm a lot more sentimental than people think."

"I'd say D," Chloe said. "If I had a boyfriend."

"You hate sewing!" Riley pointed out.

"But it's about cherishing a gift from your boyfriend," Chloe said.

"Unless he gives you a book...or his bowling trophy," Riley said. "They'd look pretty funny sewn up in a quilt."

Chloe was losing patience. "Would you answer the question?"

Riley sighed. "Okay, I'd pick C. I'd have to be honest with him."

"Okay," Chloe said, marking down their answers. She read off question number two. Then number three. The waitress brought their drinks, but Chloe put her iced mocha aside so that she could keep reading questions.

"Why don't we finish the Love Factor later?" Riley said, spooning some whipped cream from her drink. "These quizzes are so lame."

"No, no! We're almost done," Chloe insisted. "Number nine. 'Your honey lamb asks for advice about a shirt. He thinks he's decked in slammin' duds, but he's a walking, talking fashion fright. You... A. hit him with your best shot—there's power in the truth, B. break it to him gently, C. tell him that you'd love him in anything, even burlap.' "

Chloe smiled as she logged in the final answers and tallied the scores. "That makes seventy-nine points for Sierra and Larry," she said, calculating on a scrap of paper. "And..." Chloe's heart sank when she saw the score for her sister. "Forty-two for Riley and Alex."

"That's it?" Riley asked. Then she shook her head. "Well, it's no big deal," she said.

"Really?" Doubtful, Chloe watched her sister sip her iced cappuccino. The quiz said Alex was not the right boy for Riley—it had to bother her. Or at least it would bother me if I got such a low score with my boyfriend! she thought.

"I'm not worried," Riley said. "I know what I have with Alex. And those quizzes are so silly."

The front door opened with a whoosh. In walked Larry, decked out from head to ankles in a red rubber wetsuit with black stripes on the sides. His nose was caked with white sun block.

"Larry, is that you?" Riley squinted at him. "You're all...red."

"You look like an alien," Chloe added.

"Check it out, Shred Betties!" Larry said, sidling over to their table. "I just got suited up at Zuma Jay's Surf Shop."

"I love it," Sierra said, squinting at the wetsuit's blinding brightness. "You'll never have to worry about drowning. A lifeguard could spot you a mile away!"

"But what is it for?" Chloe asked. "You're not actually going surfing—are you?" She shuddered at the thought of Larry let loose on the high seas with a surfboard.

"Why not? Zuma Jay's is sponsoring a free surfing clinic this afternoon," Larry said, stealing a sip of Sierra's drink. "Anyone want to hang ten with me?"

"I've always wanted to try surfing," Riley said. "But I can't go today. I'm hanging out with Alex."

"I've got to get home soon," Sierra said. Her parents were super-strict. "Besides, Mom and Dad would never let me try surfing. Anything that might cut into violin practice time is definitely out."

"I..." Chloe looked over at the coffee bar, then snatched a copy of *Le Monde* from the newspaper rack. Lennon was headed this way. She had to look smart. "I'm going to take up French," she said.

"He's coming over!" Sierra whispered.

"I know!" Chloe whispered back, trying to act casual.

"Are you going to ask him out?" Riley asked.

"Yes!" Chloe gasped. "No!" She lowered the newspaper. "I don't know. I'll play it by ear." She tossed her long blond hair over one shoulder and leaned forward to sip her iced mocha.

Whoa! Sudden panic iced her brain. The frozen mocha was going right to her head. B*rain freeze*!

"Oh, no!" Riley gasped. "The frappe? You're frozen?" She knew Chloe's brain freeze symptoms. Whenever Chloe ate or drank something icy too quickly, her brain was paralyzed with cold!

Chloe nodded, her hands fluttering under the table. This was terrible! She couldn't think. Her head was an ice cap. No way could she have an intelligent conversation with Lennon now!

"Hey," Lennon said, pausing at their table. "How's it going, Chloe?"

chapter two

Chloe lifted a hand in a flat wave, her eyes still frozen in panic. She pressed the other hand against her nose. "O*wwwwww*!"

Lennon folded his arms across his chest. "Chloe? Are you okay?"

Chloe nodded.

"She'll be fine," Riley explained quickly. "It's a brain freeze."

"Brain freeze?" Lennon laughed. "Yeah, I sometimes have that effect on people. I freak them out. They get intimidated by my incredible wealth of knowledge. I guess it's understandable."

Oh, put a cork in it! Chloe wanted to shout. But she could only work on thawing her head.

"Brain freeze. Ha!" Lennon said, moving away toward a group of guys.

Riley gave Chloe a sympathetic look. "Is that the

worst timing, or what? Your big chance with Lennon, and your whole head ices over!"

"My fault," Chloe said in a mousy voice. She shivered. "Why do I let myself go near anything with ice?" she added.

Chloe spotted Alex Zimmer across the room, sneaking up behind Riley.

He squeezed Riley's shoulders. "Guess what? I have great news," he announced.

Riley turned around and smiled at him.

Alex's dark eyes sparkled with excitement. "We have a gig for this weekend. Friday night at Mango's!"

"What? Are you kidding me?" Sierra cried. She and Alex played together in a band called The Wave. "This weekend? Awesome!"

Alex nodded proudly. "I just talked to the manager, and we're on for Friday night. It's a solid break for the band."

"That's fantastic," Riley said, nudging Alex's arm.

As they talked out the details, Chloe turned to the coffee bar looking for Lennon. Her embarrassment was melting with her brain freeze. Now she just felt a burning challenge.

She wanted to ask him out. She wanted to get an up-close and personal look at Mr. Know-it-all. And she wanted to prove that she wasn't afraid of him.

"I'd better tell Saul," Alex said, taking out his cell phone to call the band's drummer. "He'll probably want to pull together a rehearsal this afternoon."

"There's no way I can rehearse today," Sierra said, disappointed. "I have to head home. My mom's expecting me."

"No problem," Alex told her. "I just want to try out a new song. If it works, you can learn it later in the week." Then he turned to Riley and flipped his phone closed. "Oh, Riley! I almost forgot. We were supposed to hang out this afternoon."

"No, it's okay," Riley insisted.

"We really need to rehearse," Alex said. "But I was looking forward to seeing you."

"No problem," Riley said. "I totally understand. Friday night is going to be great."

[Chloe: If I didn't know my sister so well, I'd buy that understanding bit, too. But I DO know my sister. And I can tell she's kind of disappointed.]

"Hey, Riley," Larry said. "Since you're not hanging with Alex this afternoon, that means you're free. You can come surfing with me!"

"Surfing?" Riley blinked.

Chloe smothered a laugh. Surfing with Larry was not Riley's idea of a great afternoon.

"You said you always wanted to try it, right?" Larry pointed out.

"Go for it!" Sierra said as she hitched up her backpack. "You like to try new things. And Malibu has some of the best surfing in the world."

Riley turned to Larry in his fire-engine red wetsuit.

Larry jumped onto a chair and struck a pose, arms out, as if riding a wave. "Let's ride the swells, Shred Betty!" he said.

Riley winced up at Larry's glowing red suit. "I guess..."

"Cool! Let's go!" Larry said, tugging Riley out of her chair. "We don't want to be late."

Suddenly Chloe felt a new panic. Everyone was leaving! Alex headed toward the door with his phone pressed to his ear. Larry dragged Riley. Sierra dragged her violin case.

"Hey, guys! Wait! You can't leave!" Chloe cried.

"Come with us!" Riley said.

Chloe hurried over to Riley and Sierra. "Don't leave me here alone," she whispered. "Lennon will think I'm a loser."

"But I thought you didn't like him," Riley said with a smile.

"I think I changed my mind," Chloe replied. "I'm going to make a move. Soon."

"Gotta go," Sierra said, ducking out.

"Sorry!" Riley called as Larry tugged her toward the door. "Good luck!"

That left Chloe to scurry back to the table alone. Grabbing her copy of *Teen Style*, she leaned back in the chair. Look relaxed, she said to herself. Totally cool. A girl glanced at her and Chloe smiled back as if to say: I've got it all together.

The page was still open to the Love Factor quiz. Chloe brightened. How perfect! She could take the quiz for Lennon and her.

She pulled out a purple pen and dug in. She answered question one and checked her score. The highest score possible. She answered questions two and three, then checked the answer key.

Another great score!

Her heart beat fast with excitement. She and Lennon were totally perfect for each other. She couldn't wait to finish the quiz!

With a secret smile, she looked around for Lennon. There he was, sliding his folded apron onto the coffee bar. He had his backpack on and...

Oh, no! He was leaving. His shift was ending. She had to grab him before it was too late!

Chloe dropped her pen and hurried over to the coffee bar. Forget about acting casual. This was her chance to get a date with the perfect boy for her.

Trying to pretend she wasn't nervous, she squeezed in next to Lennon at the counter. "Hey," she said.

Lennon turned away from the cappuccino machine and smiled at her. "Brain freeze over?"

"I'm totally thawed," Chloe said. Then she thought of an angle. "I didn't see you at the last party at the senior center."

"I had to go to a wedding with my parents," Lennon said.

"Hey, Lennon," one of his friends called. "Over here."

"In a minute," Lennon called, turning back to Chloe.

She was close enough to see the tiny flecks of blue in his gray eyes.

"My friends are waiting," he said.

Chloe nodded. Enough small talk, she thought. Time to pop the big Q. "So I just found out my friend Sierra is playing at Mango's," she said.

"Really?" Lennon seemed interested.

"With her band, The Wave." Chloe's heart was beating hard in her chest. She wanted to do the safe thing and stop right now, but she plunged on. "They're performing this Friday night," Chloe said, bracing herself. "And I..."

Just then, someone turned on the cappuccino machine. W*hirrrrrrr*!

It drowned out Chloe's words: "...I *was wondering if you'd like to go with me*?"

Lennon squinted, his gaze on Chloe's lips as if he was trying to read them.

Did he hear me? she wondered as the machine stopped.

Lennon nodded slowly. "That's cool," he said.

"Hey, Lennon!" his friend called again.

"Look, I have to go," Lennon said. "But we'll talk later."

"Right," Chloe said. She smiled, trying to cover her

confusion as Lennon headed off. She replayed the scene in her head as she went back to her table.

Okay, she got bonus points for asking Lennon out.

The only problem was...she wasn't sure if he'd heard her.

Did she have a date for Friday night or not?

chapter three

Riley breathed in the cool, salty mist that blew off the water. Today she was going to surf Malibu for the first time! She was going to try, anyway.

It was too bad that Alex had to cancel their afternoon together. But she'd always wanted to try surfing. And now that she was there on the beach, taking a lesson, she was glad. If only it wasn't with Larry.

Larry shuffled beside her in the sand, earphones on his head, dancing to some song playing on his Walkman. He had painted white sun-block squiggles on his cheeks. He was singing out of tune and kicking sand all over the instructor's surfboard.

Skeeter, the instructor from Zuma Jay's, waved a hand in front of Larry's face to get his attention. "Dude! Scale it down a notch."

Larry nodded, restricting his dance to a smaller area.

"Okay, surfers!" Skeeter shouted over the gentle pounding of the waves. "Place your boards flat on the sand and we'll go over the basics before you start surfing the 'Bu." The surf instructor walked along the line of students, his baggy jams and yellow T-shirt flapping in the wind.

"We're ready to hang ten, oh, mighty surf kahuna!" Larry called as he untangled his Walkman.

Skeeter lifted his shades to eye Larry.

"He's totally serious," Riley told Skeeter. "When Larry gets into something, he dives head-first."

Skeeter nodded, crossing his tanned arms in front of his chest. "Got it. Keep an eye on Larry."

Riley smiled. She felt a little like a seal in her black wetsuit with turquoise panels on the side. She slid her board onto the sand. She had rented them both at Zuma Jay's.

A guy in tropical-print swim trunks and a sleek blue surf shirt dropped his board beside hers. "Hey, you're using a fun board?"

Riley looked down at the board she'd rented. The clerk in the surf shop had recommended a fun board, since they were shorter than most, and Riley wasn't very tall. "Yeah," Riley answered. "Do you think I made the right choice? I'm a total beginner."

"Should work for you," the guy in the flowered jams said. "Not that I'm an expert or anything. But I surfed a few times in Hawaii."

"No way!" Riley cried. "If you're a hotshot, what are you doing here? This clinic is for beginners!"

The kid laughed. He had blue eyes and short-cut dark hair spiked just at the front. "I'm not that good. Actually, I stink. You'll see for yourself in a few minutes." He dropped down to the sand and stretched out on his board. "I'm Vance."

"Riley," she answered, sitting cross-legged on her own board.

"Okay, surfers," Skeeter said. He walked past the lineup of surfing students. "The main goal of this clinic is to give you the basics of surfing and to get you up on your board out there," he said, pointing toward the cresting waves.

"Cowabunga, dude!" Larry cried.

Skeeter eyed him. Riley couldn't tell if Skeeter thought Larry was funny or scary. "For starters, we're going to practice here, with your boards on the sand," Skeeter continued. "Let's have all of you stand up and take a stance on the board, one foot in front of the other."

Riley stood up on her shiny board and looked down. "Which foot goes first?" she asked.

"Good question," Skeeter replied. "It could go either way. Our stance is something that nature gives us. There's left foot in the front—that's regular. Or right foot in the front, which is called a goofy stance."

Riley looked over at Larry, who was leading with his right foot.

"Goofy stance!" Larry announced.

"Why am I not surprised?" Riley teased as she tried to find the footing that worked best for her. She stood on her board, arms out.

[Riley: Here I am...the wind gently blowing my hair back, the sun warming my skin. I'm a surf goddess, riding the crest of a wave and... Oof!]

Someone pushed her from behind!

She clambered forward, struggling for balance, and landed on the board with her left foot in front of her. She turned around to see Skeeter smiling behind her. "Hey! What was that about?" she asked.

"It's the best way to figure out your stance if you're not sure," Skeeter explained. "A sneaky push from behind always works. You're a regular."

Riley looked down at her feet. "All-righty, then. Thanks, I guess."

Next Skeeter showed them how to shift their weight to keep their balance. Riley bent her knees and gently shifted the board in the sand. It wasn't hard, but she knew it would be a different story out on the water.

Beside her, Larry toppled onto the sand. "Aw, man, I wiped out!"

"Larry, you're the first student I've ever seen wipe out before he hits the water," Skeeter said.

"Sometimes you have to learn the hard way." Larry brushed sand off his red wetsuit.

"I think you guys are about ready to get wet," Skeeter said, picking up his board. "Okay, surfers! Let's go in the water."

Riley lifted her board and ran into the foam alongside Larry and Vance. When the water was waist deep, she pushed the board under her and started paddling out.

Skeeter led the way. He paddled to a spot where half a dozen surfers lingered, waiting for a wave. Skeeter swung his board around so that he was facing the shore. "This is about far enough," he called to the group.

Riley swung her board around—and rammed right into Vance.

"Whoa! Got a license to drive that thing?" Vance asked.

"Sorry," Riley said, trying to paddle backward.

"It's okay," Vance said.

"That's one of the drawbacks of the 'Bu," Skeeter called. "Choice breaks are always going to be crowded. Now, let's get ready to take off."

Riley planted her feet on the board and looked back cautiously. A wave was rising behind her. She felt a surge of excitement as it moved closer. Still crouching, she faced the beach as her board was pulled forward.

Knees bent. Arms out. Left foot in front.

Her muscles tensed as the board wobbled beneath her. But she was moving. She was up and riding, the wave whooshing around her.

It was great! She grinned. What a thrill!

As she swirled to a stop in the shallow water, Riley threw up her hands and let out a whoop of joy. "Yes!" she shouted. She grabbed her board and turned back to the others.

Larry and Vance stumbled in the surf, picking themselves up from their wipeouts. Their boards floated nearby.

"I totally ditched!" Vance exclaimed.

"Really." Larry put a finger in one ear. "I swallowed a ton of water."

"I love this!" Riley cried. She was eager to get back and try another wave.

She paddled out with Larry and Vance and hung out in the lineup. Skeeter gave them a few tips on how to spot the perfect swell. Then Riley was off again, rising to her feet unsteadily as water churned beneath her board.

She cruised in, loving the ride!

Larry came in on the next wave, howling in excitement. "That's it for me! I'm going to go hug the sand for a while."

"Thanks for bringing me here, Larry," Riley said. "It's so great! I'm going back in."

"Later!" Larry said, dragging his board toward the beach.

Riley paddled back in and joined the other surfers. They talked as they waited in the lineup. Then suddenly, everyone was moving to catch the next wave. Riley barely noticed as an hour flew by.

Surfing *rocks*! she thought as she reached the shore once again.

"Riley?" Skeeter darted over to her, his board under one arm. "You caught another wave? Nice!"

Riley swiped the water from her cheeks. "I got lucky."

"Looks like more than luck to me," Skeeter said. "You're a natural."

His words made her feel a swell of pride. "Thanks!"

"You're welcome." Skeeter nodded. "I'm sure I'll see you around. I'm here most afternoons. Or come find me at Zuma Jay's if you want some serious lessons." He ran back into the surf and paddled out.

Vance rode past him on a wave, kneeling on his board. He made a sharp turn into the wave and flew into the water.

Riley waited for Vance on the beach, smiling. "That was some stunt," she said.

"I'm practicing for that show," he said. "The one that features Stupid Pet Tricks."

"But you're not an animal," she pointed out.

"Hey, don't blow my cover."

She nodded toward the beach. "I've got to go."

"I'll see you around," he said. "How about tomorrow? Now that you've got surf fever, you won't be able to stay away."

Riley glanced beyond him to the whitecaps and the blue horizon and the pink sunset. He was right. She couldn't wait to surf again. "See you tomorrow," she said. She plodded up the beach toward Zuma Jay's. It had turned out to be a spectacular day.

As she went to turn in her board, the clerk asked her if she'd had a good time.

Riley grinned. "It was great. In fact, how much more would it cost to keep the board for a week or so?"

The clerk smiled. "You're hooked."

Riley nodded. She couldn't wait to go surfing again. She was hooked, all right.

chapter four

"So I started taking the Love Factor quiz for Lennon, and it was amazing! We're perfect together," Chloe told her sister that evening. She couldn't stop thinking about Lennon.

"Really?" Riley pulled back her hair, still wet from the shower. "So what did you do?" They were in the kitchen, trying to keep out of Mom's way.

"I didn't even have time to finish the quiz. Lennon was leaving! So I marched right over to him and asked him out."

"Go, Chloe!" Riley said. "And...?"

"And I'm not sure he heard me," Chloe admitted, wincing. "The cappuccino machine went on at exactly the wrong time."

"But you repeated the question, right?"

"There was no time!" Chloe said. "And he just said something like 'sounds cool.' So I don't know if that means yes or whatever!"

"Oh, no." Riley frowned. "What are you going to do?"

"I don't know," Chloe answered, wringing her hands. "The whole thing is kind of embarrassing."

"Ask him again," Riley said.

"I can't." Chloe paced across the kitchen. "But maybe I have to. Oh, I don't know!"

Riley peeked through the kitchen door. "Why are we stuck in here?"

"Mom's on the phone with Milan," Chloe explained. "That show in Italy? She's talking with a seamstress who's altering Tedi's gown." Tedi was one of the main models employed by Carlson Designs, the business run by Chloe and Riley's mom.

[Chloe: Our mom isn't a noise freak or anything. We don't usually whisper around the house. But she's under a lot of pressure lately, especially since she couldn't make it to her fashion show in Italy. Dad's in Santa Fe, and they don't like to be out of town at the same time. But let me back up. Our parents are separated. They used to be fashion designers together, but then Dad decided he needed a change of pace. So he gave up designing and stress and our big house on the beach. And Mom took on the whole enchilada—all of Carlson Designs.]

"I'm starved!" Riley said, lifting the lid on a steaming pot. "Surfing really makes you hungry."

"So you liked it?" Chloe asked.

"I loved it!" Riley told her all about the lesson and Skeeter and Vance. Chloe laughed when she heard about Larry's goofy stance.

"Maybe you can get Vance together with one of your friends," Chloe whispered as their mother's voice rose out in the living room.

"I don't think so," Riley whispered back. "I mean, Sierra is into Larry, and Vance is a little too outgoing for Joelle. And I'm not sure Carrie would *get* him." She stirred the pot on the stove and licked the spoon. "Mmm...Manuelo's stroganoff." Manuelo Del Valle was the housekeeper and cook who had lived with the Carlsons since the girls were babies. Over the years, he had become a part of the family. "When's dinner?"

Chloe peeked into the living room and saw their mom pacing nervously as she spoke on the phone. "I don't think Mom's going to be eating anytime soon. There's a problem with some of the dresses."

"Oh, please, no! That could take forever! We'll be having stroganoff for breakfast." Riley stabbed a mushroom with a fork.

"Move over," Chloe said, hungry herself.

A breathless Manuelo suddenly appeared in the kitchen. "Ay! That wetsuit! It will have me up all night. I keep rushing to the patio to wet it again."

Riley shook her head. "Don't worry about it, Manuelo. As long as it's rinsed—"

"It's a wetsuit, don't you know?" he corrected Riley. "So I hose it down every half hour. I hear it's like a rhino's skin. If you let it dry, it cracks. Hopelessly ruined. Didn't you see the tag? No dry!"

Chloe held back a laugh. "I think that means don't put it in the dryer."

"I'm taking no chances," Manuelo insisted. Suddenly, he noticed the forks in the girls' hands.

Chloe shrugged. "The stroganoff is delicious."

"No touchy, touchy!" he told them. "Dinner is delayed. Your mother is on the phone. A crisis in Italy."

"Sounds like Mom's working on a diplomatic summit," Chloe said as the doorbell rang. "I'll get that."

"Would you please?" Manuelo asked. "I have gazpacho to prepare. And that suit. Oh, it's time for another wetting...." He disappeared toward the patio.

Chloe crossed the living room as quietly as possible. She opened the door and gulped.

It was Lennon!

[<u>Chloe</u>: Lennon is at my door! His eyes have little stars in them that shine only for me. He smiles that crooked smile and takes my hand. "Oh, Chloe," he says. "I just took the Love Factor quiz and I rushed right over to tell you that we belong together. We have to go out Friday night...and every weekend!" And this pink puffy cloud rises around us and lifts us into the sky and...]

"Lennon?" Chloe said in a dreamy voice.

He nodded, as if to let her know she got his name right.

Feeling like a total klutz, Chloe opened the door wider. "Come in," she said, turning to see her mom rake back her hair in distress.

"No, no, *prego*!" Macy Carlson shouted into the phone.

"Into the kitchen," Chloe whispered, ushering him past the living room. "My mom's on a call...business," she added.

Chloe stumbled and backed into the kitchen table. Lennon was here! She couldn't get over it. He was right here in her house, and she wasn't quite sure what to do with him.

Riley dropped the lid back onto the pot as she noticed them. "Hi there!" she said brightly.

"Hey." Lennon nodded at her. "Listen, Chloe, I just dropped by to give you this."

Chloe's heart began to hammer as he fumbled in his backpack. What had he brought her? A bracelet? Chocolate? Flowers?

He handed her a fat book.

"My algebra book?" she said. Her heartbeat slowed a little.

"You left it at the Newsstand," he said. "Thought you might need it."

"I do! I definitely do. Thank you," Chloe said, feeling like a babbling fool. Okay, it was only a book, but he'd brought it all the way over here. "I mean, I can't do my homework without it." It must have fallen out of my bag when I stashed away the Love Factor quiz, she thought.

"And her homework has to be done by *Friday*," Riley added, emphasizing the day. "Big day, this *Friday*."

[Chloe: Excuse me while I crawl under the kitchen table in total embarrassment. I know Riley's trying to help me. But does she have to hit Lennon over the head with the Friday thing?]

"What about you, Lennon?" Riley asked as Manuelo rushed into the kitchen muttering something about being behind schedule. "Do you have any plans for *Friday*?"

Lennon nodded. "Actually, I—"

Whi-r-r-r-r! The blender shrieked as Lennon explained his plan.

Oh, no! Chloe darted a look at the blender, where Manuelo was mixing his gazpacho. Then she stared at Lennon, trying to read his lips. But it was impossible. Hopeless!

When the noise died down, Riley stepped forward. "What was that again?" she asked Lennon.

He smiled at Chloe. "Chloe knows," he said confidently. "We talked about it this afternoon."

No, no! No, we didn't talk about it! At least, I didn't hear you! Chloe wanted to shriek. But Lennon seemed so sure of her, she couldn't admit she'd been faking all along.

She followed him to the front door helplessly, Riley trailing behind them. Mom was pacing now, though the phone was hung up.

"We got cut off," Macy explained as they passed by. "Don't touch the phone, girls. I'm waiting for them to call back."

"Hold on a minute," Riley said, catching up to Lennon and Chloe at the door. "Let's just get this straight. Right?"

Chloe nodded. This time she was glad her sister was butting in. Yes, she wanted to know Lennon's answer, once and for all.

Riley took a deep breath. "The big question is..."

Just then the phone rang.

"Are you or are you not..." Riley tried to press on, but Mom was waving frantically at them.

"Quiet, please," Macy said. "Sorry, but I have to put Tedi and the seamstress on speaker phone, so I need absolute silence."

With a silently mouthed "Bye!" Lennon ducked out the front door.

The girls leaned against the closed door and shared a look of disappointment.

Mom kneeled on the floor and leafed through an English-Italian dictionary. "How are the straps?" she asked.

"A little on the thin side," Tedi answered. "They're basically spaghetti straps."

Mom was shaking her head. "That's all wrong."

Poor Mom, Chloe thought, watching her mother fumble through the dictionary. Macy Carlson was a high-energy person, but the hectic pace of managing this show long distance was really pushing her to the limit.

"Tell her to make them thicker," she said, searching the book for a word. "Like...like..."

"Like fettuccine?" Chloe suggested.

"*Perfecto*!" Mom said, nodding at Chloe. "Did you hear that, Tedi?"

"Gotcha!" Tedi said. "And I'm worried about this rosebud. It's huge. Like a bird's nest."

"Tell her to make it small and delicate," Mom said. "Like a...a..."

"A tortellini!" Chloe called out.

"Right!" Mom said. "Did you get that?"

"It's a good thing you know pasta," Riley muttered.

Yeah, Chloe thought. Pasta was one thing she could handle. Setting up a date with Lennon was another story.

chapter five

That night Riley was dying to tell Alex about her day surfing the 'Bu. She'd found something new and wonderful that she liked to do and she wanted to share it with him.

But when she called, Alex was tied up with band rehearsal. Then there was dinner with his family. Riley knew not to call Alex at dinnertime. The Zimmers didn't like to be disturbed when they were eating. They were a little more conventional than Riley's family.

Then again, very few kids at school split their time between their mom's Malibu beach house and their dad's oceanfront trailer.

Riley's Love Factor score suddenly popped into her brain. According to the quiz, she and Alex were totally incompatible. She quessed it was true. They didn't have many of the same interests. Riley shrugged off the thought. The whole thing was stupid anyway. She didn't know why she was even thinking about it.

So we're different, Riley told herself as she sat at her computer, hoping Alex would come on-line. At least, our lives are never boring.

She was researching something for her European history homework when Alex's Instant Message flashed onto the screen.

AZIMMSTER: Wassup?

RILEY241: Surfing! I love it already!

AZIMMSTER: That's great. Did Larry survive?

RILEY241: He's still breathing. You should try it! Better than a roller coaster!

AZIMMSTER: Not into the water, remember? My sister says it's because I'm an Aries.

Riley sighed. She'd been secretly hoping that Alex would try surfing. It could be something fun they could do together.

Oh, well, she thought as a new message from Alex flashed on the screen.

AZIMMSTER: Band practice was great! We're going to really kick it up this weekend at Mango's.

No, Alex wasn't into outdoor stuff. But Riley loved to listen to him sing. And he was a great guy. So they didn't like exactly the same things. So what? He was still the boy for her.

• • •

On Tuesday morning Riley and Chloe left for school extra early. They didn't want to be around for Mom's next conference call to Italy.

Riley spotted Sierra and some other friends on the lawn outside the school building.

"Catch!" Sierra called, tossing a Frisbee at her.

Riley dropped her backpack onto a bench and ran to get the Frisbee. She tossed it back to Sierra, who was decked out in platform heels and black pants that laced up on the sides. Her red hair was twisted into tiny knots held by cute little clips.

"Hey, surfer girl! I heard you aced the clinic yesterday," Sierra said.

"I loved it," Riley admitted. "How about Larry? Was he hooked, too?"

Sierra sighed. "Larry is hanging up his surfboard and moving on. He's already into a new thing. *Teen Jeopardy*. Didn't you see him handing out these flyers in the parking lot?" She pulled a piece of purple paper from her pocket and passed it to Riley.

Riley unfolded it. "*Teen Jeopardy* tryouts will be this Friday," Riley read. She and Chloe liked the show. "That sounds like fun," Riley added.

"But there's a bonus. Did you see who's giving the three-day crash course?" Sierra asked. "Ms. Cho!"

"No way!" Riley said. Ms. Cho was one of the most popular teachers at West Malibu High.

"And the course is supposed to be a great study aid, even if you don't go on the show," Sierra said. "A great boost for scholastic exams."

"This is a must-do," Chloe said, reading over Riley's shoulder.

"Really," Riley agreed. "Where do we sign up?"

"Sign up for what?" asked a familiar voice.

Riley looked up to see Alex, his sandy blond hair catching the early-morning sun. Her heart did a little dance. "Alex, hi!" She showed him the flyer. "We were just checking out this crash course. Doesn't it look great?"

Alex nodded. "*Jeopardy*? Yeah, my parents are into that."

Sierra and Chloe headed off to play Frisbee. Riley sat on a bench. Alex dropped down beside her. "The crash course starts today after school," Riley told him. "Want to sign up with me?"

"Oh—I don't know. . . ." Alex looked away.

"What's wrong?"

His brown eyes met Riley's. "I was hoping we could do something today."

"So then come to the course, Alex!" Riley tugged on his sleeve.

He shook his head. "It's not my thing. But I wanted to see you. I mean, I was sort of hoping...but if you're into this crash thing..."

"I want to see you, too." Riley admitted. "Really.

How about if we get together after the study session?"

Alex winced. "My parents are cracking down on school nights. They're already a little bent out of shape with all the band practices."

"So when can we get together?" Riley asked. "Do I have to drag you out of rehearsal and take you to the beach?"

"And get my guitar all wet?" One corner of his mouth lifted. Almost a smile.

"You'd like surfing," Riley said.

"That made my night, thinking of you riding a wave," Alex said. "I want to come and watch you sometime. You wouldn't mind, would you?" he asked.

"No, but don't you want to try it?" Riley asked.

He shrugged. "Nah, but I'll come to the beach with you. Anytime." He leaned closer, and for a minute Riley felt herself melting under his dark eyes. "After all, you're always coming out for me whenever I play with the band. And it gives me a boost, knowing you're there," he added.

"Hey, I really love watching you play guitar. How many girls can go see their boyfriends onstage? It is so cool." Riley smiled and leaned against him, wishing things were easier.

"So are you coming Friday?" he asked.

"I wouldn't miss it!" Riley said. "But I do want to go to the crash course today."

Alex nodded. "Okay. How about tomorrow?"

"It's a three-day course. But it's only an hour tomorrow..."

"So I'll wait for you tomorrow, and we'll go over to my house together," Alex said.

"It's a deal," Riley said. She was still leaning against him, so she pushed a little harder until they both slid off the bench.

"Hey!" he laughed, pulling her back up.

Riley's hair fell into her eyes, and she smiled at him through the blond strands. "Tomorrow," she said. "Be there or be square."

"He brought the book to your house?" Amanda Gray asked Chloe.

Chloe nodded as she went through her lunch bag. Manuelo had really hit it right today. He'd packed all the cute foods that Chloe could eat with dignity. Like easy-to-pop grapes. Mineral water. (It didn't make your tongue or lips turn odd colors!) And tiny peanut-butter crackers. No crumbs, no awkward crunches. Just neat, cute food.

Today would be the perfect day to "casually" run into Lennon in the lunchroom. She glanced over at Lennon's table. Was he watching? No, at the moment he was laughing with his friends. She didn't want to get caught staring, but it was hard to look away.

"It sounds to me like the guy is into you," Amanda went on. She flipped through a magazine as she ate. "I mean, he could have just left the book for you at the school office, if he didn't care."

"Do you really think so?" Chloe asked. She popped a cracker into her mouth, still feeling a little insecure about Lennon.

"I don't understand the problem," Amanda said. "If you're not sure whether he heard you, why don't you just ask him?"

Typical Amanda. She made way too much sense. "I've tried." Chloe bit into a grape and looked at Amanda's fashion magazine. "Hey, turn to the horoscopes, will you? Maybe we can find Lennon's. I wonder when his birthday is. . . ."

Amanda turned to the horoscopes and nodded. "That's it! Here's the reason you're having trouble. Mercury is in retrograde. So, like, every sign in the zodiac is in for some problems this week." She read: "'Messages will be mixed up. Minor snafus. Nothing to worry about. Take a bubble bath!'"

"Really?" Chloe read over her shoulder. "So I just need to keep trying?" She sank back with relief. This was going to work.

"I have been so worried about this. I was beginning to think Lennon and I weren't meant to be together. But after I took the Love Factor quiz and. . ."

It hit her. She never finished the quiz!

"Oh, wow! I have to finish it!" She turned to the cover of Amanda's magazine, but she was reading *Giggle*

Girl. Chloe would have to wait until she got home to find out her final score with Lennon.

"I've heard of that quiz." Amanda brightened. "You've got to show it to me. I've been dying to take it."

"No problem," Chloe said. "I'll bring you a copy tomorrow. I can't believe I didn't finish. When I scored the first few questions, Lennon and I got a perfect score."

"Really?" Amanda blinked. "That's pretty amazing. The Love Factor is supposed to be foolproof."

Chloe nodded, watching Lennon. "I know."

Amanda followed Chloe's gaze. "You're staring at him. Why waste time? Just go right over to his table. Now's your chance if you really want to ask him."

Chloe took a sip of water. Amanda was right. What was she waiting for? She dabbed her napkin at her mouth and stood up. "I'll be right back," she told Amanda.

Feeling energized, Chloe pushed herself to *casually* walk by Lennon's table. As she listened in, Chloe realized Lennon and his friends were quizzing each other. Someone had a book of sample questions from *Teen Jeopardy*.

"The category is kings," one of Lennon's friends said. "He had six wives."

"Who is Henry the Eighth?" Lennon said without looking up from his pizza.

"Okay," someone else said. "This one is under Space

Facts. It's the only man-made structure visible from outer space."

"What is the Great Wall of China?" Lennon answered.

Lennon rattled off one answer after another. Chloe had to admit she was impressed. "Hey, Lennon," she said, acting as if she were just passing by. "Are you going to Ms. Cho's seminars?"

"No way," Lennon said. "Those things bore me. Why sit through that stuff when I already know the answers?"

Chloe cringed. This was the side of Lennon that drove her nuts. Mr. Know-it-all. "You don't seem to mind the boring questions now," she pointed out.

Lennon's friends laughed, pointing at him.

"Busted!" one kid said. "She's got you nailed."

"We're just hanging out, having lunch," Lennon said. He bit into his pizza, flashing a challenging look at Chloe.

Was he mad at her? Chloe wondered. *He* was the one who was showing off.

"Toss a few more at me," Lennon told his friends.

The boys fired off a few more questions. As Lennon answered he watched Chloe and smiled. It was as if he was teasing her.

She wished he would miss just one answer, but he got them all right. The boy knew everything. If he weren't so cute, he'd be a nerd.

Chloe felt a pang as he gave her a crooked smile.

How could she ever have fallen for him? Lennon was obnoxious with a capital O!

"Well," Chloe said, "I'm going to the crash course. I don't know everything. At least, not yet."

"Ooh!" Lennon's friends said, turning to him. "She burned you again!"

"Gee, that went well," Chloe muttered to herself as she turned away.

"Hey!" Lennon called after her. "Maybe I'll go to the crash course after all! There's got to be at least one fact I don't know!"

I doubt that, Chloe thought. She walked steadily back to the table and faced Amanda. "He's smart!" she gasped. "Really smart—and he knows it."

"So are you," Amanda said flatly. "So what's the big deal?"

Right, Chloe thought. She did well in school. Always on the honor roll.

"I get good grades," Chloe admitted, "but I don't act like I know everything. He can be so full of himself!"

"He'll get over that," Amanda said. "You'll help him get over that. Maybe Lennon just needs a girl like you to keep his ego under control."

Hmm. Chloe liked the sound of that.

"Maybe that's why you two are a perfect match," Amanda said. "You're both smart. You can teach him not to show off about it. You belong together."

Chloe popped a grape into her mouth. Maybe

Amanda was right. Maybe she and Lennon *did* belong together.

"So...are you going out with him Friday night?" Amanda asked.

"Yes," Chloe said. "Lennon might not know it yet. But we *will* go out Friday night."

chapter six

"I can't believe it," Riley whispered to Sierra as they entered the auditorium for the *Teen Jeopardy* crash course. "Vance is here. I told you about him. He's my surfing buddy from yesterday."

"Really?" Sierra looked around. "Where?"

Riley nodded toward him. "He's by the flag. Short black hair. Nice tan. Blue eyes."

"You didn't mention that he was totally hot," Sierra whispered.

"I didn't—" Riley stopped herself as she got her first real look at Vance. She liked his easy smile and the way he wore his short brown-black hair spiked over his forehead. Okay, she had noticed his pale blue eyes before. But somehow the whole package didn't register with her until now.

Vance was gorgeous.

"Wow, he really is cute," she murmured.

"Told you," Sierra said. "And you're just noticing? Where've you been?"

Riley shrugged. "Since I already have a boyfriend, I guess it didn't cross my mind."

Sierra's eyebrows shot up as she gave Riley a curious look. "I'm crazy about Larry, but I can still appreciate a hottie when I see one."

Riley turned away from Vance and tried to focus. She hadn't expected to see him here. She didn't even know he went to West Malibu High. "How weird is that? I never noticed the guy before, and now, twice in two days, I run into him."

"Life is full of random weirdness," Sierra said. "Speaking of weirdness, there's my cutie." She pointed across the room.

Larry bounced up and down, waving them over to seats he'd saved.

The girls went to sit with Larry as Ms. Cho called for the meeting to start. "Let's jump right in," Ms. Cho said. "Today we're going to do drills. That means we need to break into smaller teams. I will assign them so that we don't all end up with our best friends. Okay?"

As the teacher went down the rows giving out numbers, Riley hoped she could be on Sierra's team. But what were the chances?

"Okay, let's have all the ones here, all the twos here," Ms. Cho said, assigning areas to the different teams.

When Riley went to find her teammates, there was Vance. It gave her a funny feeling in the pit of her stomach. Sort of giddy. Nervous. Excited.

Riley bit her lower lip. What was that about? It wasn't as if she liked Vance or anything—was it?

"I'll race you up the hill!" Riley called, pedaling her bike hard.

"You'll never beat me!" Vance challenged, switching gears. "If you pull ahead, I'll just crack you up again."

Riley could barely pedal, she was laughing so hard. Vance had just told her a funny story about how he'd once ditched his bike in a puddle of melted ice cream.

After the crash course ended, Sierra and Larry left together, and Riley found herself walking to the bike rack with Vance. He'd biked to school that day, just as she had. He talked her into taking a detour, since it was such a beautiful day. They rode up the paved path that wound along Malibu beach.

As they pedaled over the rise of the hill, the ocean came into view. The sun was low, hiding behind pink clouds that hung over the sparkling blue water of the Pacific. She wished that Alex were here to share it, but then, he wasn't really into riding bikes.

"You can stop pedaling, Riley," Vance called. "I give up. Victory is yours."

She cruised to a stop and stepped off the seat. "Check out that sky."

Vance circled, then braked beside her. "Yeah, everything looks awesome from up here. Too bad we don't have time to hit the beach."

"I want to go surfing tomorrow," Riley said. "But not today—it'll be dark soon. Besides, I have too much homework."

"Me, too," Vance said. "I've got algebra assignments coming out my ears. Maybe we should get started on it. There's a pizza place up ahead with outdoor tables. We could crack open the books and knock off our homework. And I wouldn't mind grabbing a slice."

It sounded like a good idea to Riley. "Let's go," she said, swinging onto her bike again.

They cruised along until they came to a stretch of beach with a café, a bookstore, and a pizza parlor. Vance ordered two slices and sodas. Then they cracked open their books and got to work.

"I do okay with this stuff," Vance said as he scratched out an equation. "But I don't see how I'm ever going to need it. Not with what I want to do."

"And that is...?"

"Professional snowboarding." His blue eyes lit up. "Have you ever tried it? It's my ultimate favorite sport. Especially the stunts. Flips and spirals."

"I've skied in Tahoe a few times," Riley said. "But I've never flipped down the slope. At least, not on purpose," she added.

"You have to try it!" Vance said. "My dad got me into

it. He's works in an office, so he loves tearing out of there on long weekends. And I've got this wild uncle who loves camping and stuff. We go kayaking and hiking. Surfing and skiing. Depending on the weather."

"Sounds great," Riley said, chewing her pencil. She had a lot of fun with Vance, biking and surfing...and even at the crash course today. Vance had managed to psych up everyone on their team. He taught them some tricks to help them remember the presidents, the planets in the solar system, the periodic table of elements.

Their bubbling hot pizza arrived. Riley took a bite and thought about all the active, outdoorsy things she enjoyed doing, like hiking and swimming and surfing. It had been ages since she went camping or hiking. Why had she been hanging back lately?

[Riley: I almost choked on my pizza when it hit me. Alex! Not that he stops me from biking or swimming...but Alex isn't into those things. So we usually hang out at his house or walk along the beach. It's nice. We have a great time together. Really. But sometimes I miss doing all those other things, too.]

Vance talked about canoe trips he'd taken with his dad. Riley listened as she ate her pizza. She laughed at Vance's stories and watched as the sun set over the ocean, all pink and purple and gold.

It was sort of the perfect date. Sort of.

Because it wasn't really a date at all. And Riley was still crazy about Alex.

Really, Riley thought as Vance leaned close to help her with an algebra equation. Vance is just a friend!

"I can't believe I skipped the crash course to chase a guy," Chloe said as the waitress delivered three coffee frappes to their table.

[Chloe: Correction: two frappes and one hot latte. I made one important promise to myself yesterday. No more cold drinks in front of Lennon. At least, not until our third date!]

Chloe enlisted the advice of her other good friends Tara Jordan and Quinn Reyes. And they convinced her that if she wanted to zero in on Lennon, she had to report to the Newsstand immediately. As Tara pointed out, it was already Tuesday. If Chloe was to finalize her plans for Friday, she had to get an answer from Lennon.

"Believe it," Tara said.

"Come on, Chloe," Quinn pointed out. "Do you want to go out with Lennon or not?"

"I do, I do—I think," Chloe said, taking a sip of her warm latte. "You should have seen him in the lunchroom, spouting off answers to those quiz questions. The guy is a brain wrapped in a hottie package." Chloe shook her head. "He's way too perfect. Except for the fact that *he knows* he knows everything."

"Well, you'd better figure out how you feel about Mr. Perfect pretty fast," Quinn whispered. "Because he just came out of the kitchen."

Chloe swallowed hard as she turned toward him. She didn't want to like the boy genius—she just couldn't help it!

"Oh, Chloe," Tara said, shaking her head. "You've got it bad, girl."

"I must be crazy," Chloe said.

"Okay, you're crazy," Quinn said as Lennon went to talk with some of his friends. They had taken a table near the newspaper rack, and they were joking about headlines. "Now go talk to him. Find out exactly what he's doing Friday night."

Chloe stood up and straightened her ruffled shirt. "Right. I can do this. It's a simple question, right?"

"Right!" her friends answered.

Marching over to Lennon's table, Chloe felt a sudden stab of panic. What was she going to say?

[Chloe: At times like this, I can count on my brain to come up with mush. Just take a look at my conversation starters: 1. Did anyone ever tell you that you look hot in an apron? 2. Did anyone ever tell you that you're incredibly obnoxious? 3. Did anyone ever tell you that you're the guy for me?]

Okay, maybe those were all the wrong things to say. She should focus on Friday night. But that seemed so blunt.

Suddenly hesitant, she squeezed her toes around her flip-flops as she reached Lennon and his friends.

"Hey, Chloe," Lennon said, looking up from a newspaper.

"Hi!" Chloe said. The word flew out of her mouth like a lone moth, and that was it. Empty. Nothing else to say.

"What does that one say?" one of his friends asked Lennon, who was holding a copy of a French newspaper called *Le Monde*.

"The headline is about a demonstration in Marseilles," Lennon answered. "And this is a story about how little snow they've had in the French Alps."

"Cool," another boy said. He shoved a different paper at Lennon. "What's this?"

"It's German, from Stuttgart," Lennon answered. "The lead story is about...how they're opening a new factory to make Porsches."

"Wow, is there any language you don't speak?" someone asked.

Lennon rolled his eyes. "Plenty! I just picked up a lot when my family moved around Europe. But I'd be lost in China or the Middle East."

Was that a flash of modesty from the brilliant Lennon? Chloe wondered. Maybe he wasn't a totally stuck-up snob.

"Pretty impressive," she admitted, thinking of how she'd struggled with Spanish until Manuelo had started coaching her.

As the guys shoved other newspapers at Lennon, Chloe's gaze landed on a photograph of Tedi.

"Whoa!" She pulled the paper toward her.

"You know her?" Lennon asked.

"That's Tedi, the main model for my mom's label. Mom's a designer," Chloe said. "And this Italian show has been really hard for her."

Chloe thought of the crunch Mom had been under with this latest show. Talk about stress! Mom had been up most of the night, worrying over design changes.

She studied the headline. Since it was an Italian newspaper, the only thing she could decipher was Tedi's name in the caption. "I wonder what this is about."

Lennon leaned closer. "Good press for Carlson Designs," he said. "It says that Tedi is one of the beautiful models in Milan for the fall show. Actually, it says she *is* the most beautiful."

An idea buzzed in Chloe's mind. "You speak Italian?"

Lennon nodded. "Sì."

If Lennon spoke Italian, he could help Mom! There wasn't a moment to lose. Mom needed him to translate. She was probably struggling through an overseas phone call right now.

Without another thought, Chloe grabbed his arm and gave a tug. "Why didn't you say so! My mom has been going nuts trying to talk to Italian seamstresses! She needs you desperately!"

"I'd like to help," Lennon said. "But I'm not totally fluent. I just know a few words."

"That's more than Mom knows," Chloe said, tugging on his arm. "You've got to come with me. Now!"

chapter seven

"Let's move on to the evening gown," Macy Carlson said with authority.

Lennon translated for the seamstresses on the other end of the speakerphone.

Macy turned to Chloe, who put down the sketch of the suit she'd been holding and grabbed the sketch Mom needed.

This is going great! Chloe thought.

With Lennon translating, Mom was free to think about the design. Even Chloe was able to help, finding the right sketches and measurements so that Mom could focus on the most important thing—perfecting the details. Working as a team, the three of them had made it through alterations on most of the Carlson collection.

Chloe grinned. She liked being on Lennon's team. When he wasn't trying to impress his friends, Lennon was a great guy.

"Is the bodice snug enough?" Mom asked.

"It fits like a glove," Tedi answered. "I'm just not sure about this hemline. It goes up in front."

Chloe sifted through the sketches to find the dimensions of the gown. She handed them to her mom.

"It should rise a little," Macy answered. She looked down at the notes Chloe had found. "Just enough to reveal some toe cleavage."

Lennon translated for Mom, and the seamstress shot back another question in Italian.

Chloe listened carefully, trying to anticipate Mom's next move. This was fun! Not that she was totally obsessed with high fashion or anything, but the air was crackling with excitement.

"I've decided to make it pasta night, in honor of your show," Manuelo announced from the kitchen door. "Four different types. Spaghetti, radiatori, percatelli..."

"Shh!" everyone hushed him.

"Oh! Sorry!" Manuelo's hand flew to his mouth. "I thought you were finished."

"Now...where were we?" Mom asked.

"The hemline," Chloe said, pointing to the sketch. Now she was the one keeping Mom on track. That was a switch!

"Right. Is the hemline falling properly in the front?" Mom asked. "It shouldn't buckle around the seam."

As Lennon translated, the door opened and Riley breezed in. "Hey, everybody!" she said cheerfully.

"Shh!" Manuelo said. "Can't you see they're in conference?"

"But we're almost finished," Chloe said quietly.

Manuelo threw up his hands and returned to the kitchen.

As Lennon and Mom talked, Riley edged over to Chloe. "What's going on?" she asked.

"Lennon is translating," Chloe whispered. "He knows Italian. Can you believe it?"

"How great is that?" Riley said.

"It's totally great!" Chloe tried to keep from bubbling over with excitement.

"I think that covers everything," Tedi said over the phone. "And it's a good thing. I'm walking down the runway tomorrow."

"That's it," Mom said, raising a fist in victory. "We did it! Call me if you need me, Tedi."

"Will do," Tedi said. "*Ciao, bella.*"

Mom swept the design board out of Chloe's hands and danced her around the room. "*Finito*! I am so relieved! Now I can collapse and watch that Daffy Duck marathon on the Cartoon Network."

"I didn't know there was a Daffy marathon today," Lennon said. "I love Daffy Duck! He and Elmer Fudd are my favorites."

"Elmer is good, too," Mom said. "But nothing beats twelve straight hours of Daffy."

Chloe stared from Lennon to Mom and back again.

Was this really happening? Was the boy she liked bonding with her mom in one easy step? She wanted to rush forward and throw her arms around both of them.

No...that would be a little pushy. First she should get a date with Lennon. T*hen* she would throw her arms around him.

"And Lennon," Mom went on, "thank you so much! My show would never have been ready in time without you."

"Yes, thanks, Lennon," Chloe said. "You were awesome. Especially when that seamstress shot back questions in rapid-fire Italian."

Lennon gestured around the room. "We make a great team. By the way, what in the world is toe cleavage?"

Chloe and Riley looked down at their own flip-flops and started laughing. "You don't want to know," Chloe teased Lennon. "It's definitely not a guy thing."

Lennon laughed.

He's so nice! Chloe thought. How could I ever have thought he was a snob?

Mom gathered up the sketches. "Manuelo, I'll be parked in front of my cartoons."

"Dinner in ten minutes, Mrs. Macy," Manuelo called from the kitchen. "That gives you time for one episode of Daffy."

"I guess I'd better get going," Lennon said.

As Chloe walked him to the door, she thought of

how much had changed in the past hour. She'd seen a deeper side of Lennon, and his talent with languages had made Mom's day. She followed him out the door to put the perfect ending on the afternoon.

Chloe pulled the door closed behind her. Suddenly they were face-to-face. Chloe felt the electricity between them. She couldn't help staring at the little flecks of blue in his pale gray eyes. A warm feeling swept over her as he reached out and touched her arm.

"I'm glad you brought me home with you, Chloe," he said. "I had a good time."

Chloe felt herself melt. "Me, too. Thanks."

"Anytime," Lennon said. Then he turned to head up the beach road. "See you tomorrow."

"Bye!" Chloe waved after him, deciding to wait until he was gone to break into her happy dance. She had dragged Lennon to her house. He had said they made a great team. How hard could it be to coordinate a date for Friday?

Friday! She almost forgot.

"Oh, wait. Lennon?" she called.

Just then a jet plane passed overhead with a loud rumble.

"Lennon! Are we...?" But Chloe's voice was totally drowned out by the noise. "You've got to be kidding me," she muttered as Lennon disappeared around a corner.

Frustrated, she headed back into the house. For two

people who are supposed to be a perfect match this was getting pretty weird. Why was it so difficult to find out if they had a date?

Then Chloe remembered something even more urgent. The Love Factor quiz! She had to finish it!

chapter eight

Riley stretched out on her rosebud quilt to do her homework. She opened her algebra book. Duh! How could she forget? She'd already finished her algebra with Vance at the pizza place.

She closed the book and laughed, remembering how Vance had talked his way through the algebra problems. He pretended the variables were spies. "I'm going to neutralize you, Agent X," he'd said. "I'll find out your equal, Agent Y."

It was goofy, but she liked it.

Just then the bedroom door burst open. "You're never going to believe this!" Chloe announced, beaming. "Not in a million years!"

Riley lifted her head. "What?"

"Lennon and I aced the quiz!" Chloe bounced onto the bed beside Riley.

Riley tried to focus on the copy of *Teen Style* that

Chloe shoved in front of her face, but the whole bed was jiggling from Chloe's bouncing.

"You're making me seasick!" Riley said, gripping the magazine. "You took the Love Factor quiz?"

Chloe nodded. "And we totally maxed out on every question!"

"I had a feeling," Riley said. "He seemed pretty comfortable helping Mom this afternoon, too."

"Didn't he?" Chloe hugged the magazine to her chest, then tossed it onto the bed. "This is so great! I'm not going to let anything else get in the way. I'm calling him right now!"

Just then the phone rang, and Riley laughed. "Well, if the Love Factor is right, that's probably Lennon calling *you* right now!"

Hopeful, Chloe grabbed the phone, and said hello. "Oh, hi, Alex," she said. "Sure, she's here. Hold on." She handed the phone to Riley, saying, "I'll use the business line downstairs."

Chloe left, and Riley pressed the phone to her ear. "Hi! How's it going?" she asked, looking down at her math notebook. She noticed a little doodle Vance had scribbled on a page. A silly face with a mustache. Feeling a pang of guilt, Riley quickly closed the notebook and turned around.

"I'm great," Alex said. "What did you do this afternoon?"

"I..." She choked on the words. Why was he asking

that? Had he heard something? "I...nothing special. I went for a bike ride. Homework. Things like that."

As Alex told her about a history project he was working on, Riley wondered why she didn't tell him about Vance. It was an innocent thing. But it would sound as if she was making a big deal out of it. Wouldn't it? And it would only underline the fact that Alex didn't like to go biking or surfing....

"What did you end up doing after school?" she asked him, hoping to change the subject.

"The usual. I played guitar a while. Came up with half a song. Played it for Saul over the phone."

"Did he like it?" Riley asked.

"He's cool with it," Alex answered. "It still needs work, though."

"Uh-huh." Riley bit her lower lip. She didn't know what to say next. Sometimes phone conversations with Alex were like that.

"So how was that whole *Teen Jeopardy* thing?" Alex asked her.

"Really fun," Riley told him. "We learned a cool trick to memorize the presidents and the planets and constellations. I know it sounds boring, but Ms. Cho makes it interesting."

"Yeah," Alex said. He had Ms. Cho for social studies. "She's great."

Riley took a deep breath, trying to get past the tight feeling in her chest. "Well..." She tried to think of something else to talk about, but suddenly her afternoon with Vance weighed on her mind. His face loomed there, reminding her of the good time they'd had together after school.

She just couldn't tell Alex about it.

"I guess I'd better go," she said. "I've got a bunch of presidents to memorize."

Riley clicked off the phone and let her head drop onto the bed. She felt so awful! She hated hiding anything from Alex.

Chloe burst in again with an update. "Okay, I called Lennon, and he was home! But someone beeped in, and it was a call his dad had to take. So he's calling me back."

"Great!" Riley said. She really was happy things were working out for Chloe, but she couldn't shake her bad feeling.

"What's the matter?" Chloe asked.

"It's nothing," Riley said.

"What?" Chloe pounced onto Riley's bed. "What happened between you and Alex? I can tell something is wrong. Tell me!"

"Nothing happened with Alex," Riley admitted. "It's Vance."

"The surfer boy?" Chloe asked.

Riley nodded. "He turned up at the *Teen Jeopardy* crash course today. He landed on my team. And when the course was over, we walked out together. We ended up going on a bike ride. Then we stopped at this pizza place to do our homework."

"So?" Chloe shrugged. "Sounds innocent enough. What are you so worried about?"

Riley sighed. Chloe was right. It was no big deal. Vance was a cool guy, and Riley liked to hang out with him. So what? Why should she feel guilty?

"Alex is your boyfriend," Chloe said. "But you're still allowed to talk to other guys."

"I know," Riley said. "That's why I don't understand why I'm afraid to tell Alex about Vance. Does it mean something?"

"Let's see what *Teen Style* has to say about this," Chloe said, leafing through the magazine. "According to the Love Factor, you don't need to feel guilty if—"

"Chloe?" Riley interrupted. "Can we just forget the quiz? I can't get into it right now."

"Okay," Chloe agreed. "You need to do what's right for you. I mean, just because the Love Factor worked for Lennon and me..." She put the magazine aside and jumped up. "I've got to go call Tara and Quinn. They're going to freak when they hear about my incredible score!"

Chloe left, and Riley flopped down on the bed.

That dumb quiz! At least Chloe was happy about it.

But if Riley believed the Love Factor's scores, she and Alex were in trouble. Which was ridiculous, since everyone knew they got along just fine.

The magazine sat on her nightstand, practically

calling at her to open it and take the quiz again. I shouldn't, she thought. It will only confuse me more.

She could hear Chloe's voice in her head. "The Love Factor is foolproof!"

With a deep breath, Riley sat up and grabbed the magazine. She didn't believe in the quiz. Not really. But it was tempting.

She could take it again...this time for Vance. Just to see how they did together.

No, that was silly.

She glanced at the first question. "'Your love gives you a gift wrapped with a big fat bow!'" she read aloud.

Oh, why not?

"Tara thinks I should call Lennon back," Chloe said as she burst into the bedroom a few minutes later.

Riley dropped her pencil and shoved her score sheets under the magazine. Caught! Even though she wasn't doing anything wrong. But she didn't want Chloe to know she was taking the quiz *twice*.

"But Quinn has a different theory," Chloe went on, leaning into the mirror to unhook her shell necklace. "She thinks that forces may be keeping us apart. Supernatural forces."

"I don't know about that." Riley frowned. "A noisy jet and a whirring blender wouldn't really make it on *The X-Files*."

"But you've got to admit it's weird." Chloe turned

away from the mirror and sat across from Riley. Her gaze fell on the open magazine.

Riley squirmed.

"What's this?" Chloe reached over and slid out the two pages of answers in Riley's handwriting. "Riley? Two sets of answers? You took the Love Factor quiz over again?"

Riley winced. "I was just goofing around with it. I didn't finish," she admitted, hoping Chloe would just forget about it. "No big deal."

"So go on and finish it!" Chloe insisted, looking at the papers. "This one is done, and this one..." She blinked. "You took the test with Vance as a boyfriend?"

Riley winced again. "I told you, I was just goofing around."

"So finish!" Chloe repeated. "We've got to see how this works out."

Biting her lower lip, Riley finished the last three questions and handed Chloe the answer sheet.

Chloe nodded as she scored Riley's answers. "Nice score! This is great. It says you are a great match for...Vance!"

Riley blinked. "Vance? But what about Alex?"

"Not so great with him," Chloe admitted. "But you knew that already."

Uh-oh, Riley thought.

"I think you know what this means," Chloe said.

Riley hugged her knees. "I was kind of afraid of this,"

she admitted. "But I guess...maybe...I like Vance. As more than friend. At least a little."

"What are you going to do?" Chloe asked.

"I don't want to do anything to hurt Alex," Riley said. "So I guess, starting tomorrow, I'll just have to stay away from Vance."

chapter nine

"Chloe, the gig at Mango's is the day after tomorrow," Quinn said on Wednesday morning at school. "And you still don't know for sure if Lennon is going there with you."

"You have to act," Tara ordered. "Now."

"I know," Chloe moaned. "He never called me back last night! No matter how hard I try to pin him down, something always gets in the way."

"Well, you can't let *him* get away." Quinn sat on the step beside Chloe. "Lennon is major boyfriend material."

She reached into Chloe's backpack and flipped open Chloe's cell phone.

"What are you doing?" Chloe asked.

Tara held out a slip of paper with a number on it. "Lennon's cell phone," she said.

"He has a cell phone?" Chloe snatched the paper. "How did you get this number?"

"Never mind that," Tara said. "He's only supposed to use the phone for emergencies. But this definitely qualifies. Now dial. He's probably on his way to school."

Quinn handed her the cell phone. "Call him. Ask him. Do it now."

"Okay, okay!" Chloe tapped in the cell number and waited as it rang. She bit her lower lip. "He's not answering," she said. "And I'm not getting voice mail."

"Maybe he's on the other line," Tara said.

Quinn frowned. "Still ringing?"

Chloe held out the phone so Quinn could hear. "No go." An image flashed through her mind—Lennon the show-off, shooting off answers to quiz-show questions in the cafeteria. She felt annoyed. "He's probably on the other line with some girlfriend in Sweden. Some girl he can actually connect with. Because that's Lennon, the big, important world traveler. Mr. Know-it-all."

"Chloe?" There was a voice on the line. Lennon's voice.

Chloe gasped. When had the ringing stopped? How much had he heard?

She pressed the phone to her ear.

"Is that you?" he asked.

Panicked, Chloe pressed the button to hang up. "I blew it!" she moaned.

"What happened?" Tara shrieked.

"Did he answer?" Quinn asked.

Chloe nodded.

"Did he hear you?" Tara asked. "*What* did he hear?"

"I don't know!" Chloe moaned. "It took him such a long time to answer the phone. I figured he was never going to pick up."

"It's okay," Tara said. "You are totally covered. He has no way of knowing it was you."

"Right," Chloe said, nodding. "Except that I think he recognized my voice. He said my name." She pressed her chin against her fist. "I am so busted."

I have total willpower, Riley thought. I'm in complete control.

She looked up from her history book and glanced around the library. She'd made it all the way to study period without running into Vance once.

I can do this, she told herself. She chewed her pencil. If she stayed away from Vance, she would have no problem. Soon she'd forget how much fun she had with him and stop liking him.

Yes, that was the plan. Now if only she could stop thinking about him and focus on her work.

Okay...back to the Battle of 1812.

"Riley! Hey!" Vance waved to her and walked across the library, straight for her table. He grabbed a chair and sat down.

Riley grinned. So much for willpower.

"How's it going?" Vance said. "I just got a mondo paper assigned in social studies. I like to get that stuff out of the way during study period. I mean, who needs to be doing homework after school when you can get out and bike and surf and stuff?"

"Totally." Riley nodded.

"So, do you mind if I study with you until next period?" Vance asked.

"Um—no, I don't mind," Riley replied. What could she say? No, you can't study with me? No, this library is for my personal use only?

This is ridiculous, she thought. How can I avoid someone who goes to the same school as I do? And why should I? Vance is a fun guy and I like to hang out with him. So what?

"So what are you doing after school?" Vance asked.

"I've got the *Jeopardy* course," Riley said. They were on the same team. There was no way she could avoid him there. But that wasn't her fault, was it?

"Oh, right! So do I." Vance nodded. "How about after that? Do you want to hang out?"

Yes! Yes, I do, Riley thought. But... "I can't," she said. She had plans with Alex.

"Oh." Vance was scribbling something in his notebook. "How come?"

She hesitated. Should she mention Alex?

"Too much homework," she said. *Chicken*, she scolded herself.

"Tell me about it," he said. "Sometimes I think the teachers just want to torture us. Maybe all this homework is a plot to keep us busy while the teachers secretly try to take over the world."

Riley laughed. "Somehow I can't see Mr. Vargas running the world." Mr. Vargas was a science teacher. He had very thick glasses and tiny little teeth like yellow Chiclets.

"No, see, he's got a great cover," Vance said. "You'd never suspect somebody with glasses that thick. But underneath he's a villain right out of a spy movie. He definitely gives the most homework, anyway."

Riley laughed again. Before she knew it, study period was over—and she hadn't gotten much studying done.

chapter ten

I haven't seen Alex all day, Riley thought as she settled at her desk in Mr. Bender's English class. That's strange. She usually had lunch with him on Wednesdays. But Riley had just finished lunch, with no sign of Alex.

R*rrrrrriiiiiinnnnnggg*! The fire alarm blared through the school. Fire drill!

"Leave your books where they are," Mr. Bender said. "Proceed out the door to the left. Single file!"

Riley hurried out of the classroom. Another line of students marched down the hall. She walked alongside them, keeping an eye out for Alex.

"This is all part of the plot," a familiar voice said in her ear. "Fire drills, I mean."

Riley turned around. Vance!

"While we're all outside learning about fire safety, Mr. Vargas is in the chemistry lab, cooking up some kind of secret potion," Vance said.

"Yeah, a mind-control potion," Riley said, going along with the joke. "He'll take over the school. First West Malibu High, then the world!"

They laughed as they headed down the outdoor stairs of the annex. Riley stared at the sea of students assembling on the school lawn.

Where was Alex? Why didn't *he* run into her during the fire drill?

Riley liked hanging with Vance, but this was getting crazy. How could she avoid him when he seemed to pop up everywhere?

At last! Chloe thought when she spotted Lennon in the hallway. She was late for science class, but she didn't care. Now was her chance to clear the air once and for all. Did she have a date with Lennon on Friday night or not? And did he hear what she said about him over the cell phone? Was he mad at her?

"Lennon!" she called. He stopped and turned around. "I've got to ask you something—"

R*rrrrriiiiiinnnnnggg*! The fire alarm clanged. Chloe couldn't believe it. How could this be happening *again*?

"We'd better get out of here," Lennon said as the classroom doors popped open around them.

Chloe sighed and followed him down the hall. Major humiliation! Maybe it was fate. Maybe it was her destiny *not* to be with Lennon.

At least he didn't mention the phone call.

"Sorry I didn't get back to you last night," Lennon said. "My dad's business call took forever."

"That's okay," Chloe said. She wondered if she should apologize about the cell phone hang up. No, don't go there, a little voice warned her. Instead, she changed the subject. "Tedi called back last night to ask about our mysterious translator. All the seamstresses in Milan want to meet you."

Lennon laughed. "How did your mother's show go?" he asked.

"Actually, it should be starting any minute," she said, "and without any problems, thanks to you."

The bell rang. That was the signal to return to class.

"I'm going to stop by my locker," Lennon said. "Catch you in bio."

I hope so, Chloe thought as she turned toward the lab. I hope you catch every word I say to you! Because biology was the only class they had together. It was time to make her move. She passed a bulletin board covered with flyers and notices.

The power of the written word. Maybe that was the way to go. That's it! she thought. I'll put my question in writing. What could be more definite than that?

She would write him a note. Then, at least, she would know whether the answer was yes...or no.

There was no time to lose. Definitely no time to run the note by Tara and Quinn. Chloe would have to make the pass during science class. That was the only time she was guaranteed to see Lennon. She opened her notebook and thought about what to write. Something short and sweet. To the point. A no-frills note. She took out her purple pen and wrote:

Are we on for Friday night?
–Chloe

She thought about a border. Maybe some stars and hearts?

No, she decided. Keep it simple. She folded up the paper and tucked it into the pocket of her Capri pants. She was ready....

She walked into the biology classroom. Half the class was already there, sitting on stools at the high counters in the lab area, adjusting their goggles. Oh, no! It was a lab day!

Oh, great! She was going to have to confront Lennon wearing steamed-up goggles and smelly latex gloves. Way to look cute.

"Let's settle in as quickly as possible," Mr. Levine, the teacher, said. "We're going to dissect sea anemones today, and it will take the entire period."

"Gross!" Chloe took her seat next to Amanda, her lab partner. Mr. Levine came around with a huge jar of the spiny creatures. "They smell terrible!"

"That's the formaldehyde," Amanda said. "It's, like, a preservative."

"Couldn't they add a little perfume to that stuff?" Chloe said, pressing the goggles against her nose.

The class settled in as Mr. Levine began his instructions.

"I need a favor," Chloe whispered to Amanda. She reached into her pocket, trying to play it cool. Like most teachers, Mr. Levine was not a fan of note-passing. "Pass this on for me. To Lennon."

Amanda nodded. She took the note and slid it along the black countertop. It zipped past Matthew Kazorowski and stopped right in front of Lennon. Perfect! Amanda was a pro.

"Thank you!" Chloe whispered.

But Lennon was focused on Mr. Levine and didn't see the note. Matthew spotted it, though. He reached over and flicked it with his forefinger.

The folded note skittered across the counter, back toward Chloe. A perfect table-hockey puck.

"No!" Chloe muffled the word as she reached out to snatch it. The note bounced off her arm and glided over to Mike Malone.

Mike grinned and shot it back across the shiny black counter.

"Stop it!" Chloe hissed in a panic.

But the guys were too amused to listen. The note went to Preston Phillips. Then back to Matthew. Then Mike. Then over to Preston, who shot it off the counter.

"That's it," Chloe muttered, slipping off her stool to

go and recover the note. She snatched it off the floor and returned to her seat, feeling discouraged. She would have to abandon her mission. When it came to communicating with Lennon, she couldn't seem to do anything right!

She set the note on the counter in front of her. Maybe she could catch Lennon at the end of class when he was on his way out the door.

She sighed and turned her attention to Mr. Levine and the sea anemones. But then, out of the corner of her eye, she sensed movement nearby. She glanced down at the note. A hand covered it and plucked it off the counter.

Chloe's gaze moved past the hand, up the arm, and rested on the pimply face of Dylan Greenley. He was sitting across the counter from her, clutching the note.

What was he doing? She didn't know him well, only that he was shy and sort of nerdy. Totally into video games. He carefully unfolded the note and read it.

Oh, no, Chloe thought. She began to panic. Dylan thought the note was for him!

"Friday night?" Dylan smiled, and Chloe squinted in the major solar flash from his braces. "Sure!" he said.

Chloe swallowed hard. This couldn't be! But there was Dylan, refolding her note.

"Okay," Chloe said, nearly choking on the word.

Across the table, Lennon was watching. What could she do?

She could barely get the words out. "Then we're on for Friday, Dylan."

Chloe picked up her scalpel with a sigh. Somehow, cutting up a smelly sea creature didn't seem so gross now. It was a lot more appealing than her current social life.

chapter eleven

"How's the *Jeopardy* thing going?" Alex asked as he set a plate of cheese and crackers on the table.

"Great!" Riley settled into a corner of the basement couch. She was glad to see Alex at last, glad to be at his house, glad that the day was over. "I'm learning a lot and Ms. Cho makes it fun." She didn't add that Ms. Cho had tried a different format that day, with different teams. That left Vance on the opposite side of the room, far, far away. When the course ended, Riley had ducked out the side door and dashed off to meet Alex in the school library.

And now here she was, settling in with Alex. He popped a cube of cheese into his mouth, swung his guitar onto his lap, and started picking out a melody.

"Well, I'm glad we could get together today," Alex said. "Between my band practice and your *Teen Jeopardy*, things were looking kind of dismal there."

She smiled. He'd missed her.

"Hey," Alex said, "let me play you the new song I've been working on."

Munching a cracker, Riley watched him intently as he sang.

"*Through a window, see her there. Through a doorway, lost somewhere. Listen closely for the sound. Feel the silence. Look around.*" His fingers moved over the neck of the guitar, picking out a riff.

Riley nodded, waiting for more.

"That's all there is right now," he said. "I'm still working on a bridge."

"It's great," Riley said. "How do you come up with such creative lyrics?"

"They usually just pop into my mind," he admitted. "But sometimes I have to keep working them. Over and over." He picked up a cracker. "You must get bored, hanging out in a basement, listening to me practice."

"No! I love it," Riley said as he started playing a familiar song. It was the one he wrote for her.

"*Pass her in the hall...Try to catch her smile,*" he sang, his eyes on her. "*Don't you know you're all I need for a while?*"

She leaned back into the worn couch and watched Alex, her heart swelling. Sure, she liked Vance, but she liked Alex, too. They were like two different sides of her, the quiet and the adventurous.

Everything seemed so complicated—more complicated than anything a teen magazine quiz could handle.

• • •

Riley walked home from Alex's house along the ocean path, feeling good. It was a beautiful afternoon, and the sun still had a few hours to go before it set. As she approached the Malibu beach near her home, she spotted a few kids out surfing.

What a great idea!

She decided to rent a board at Zuma Jay's, then jogged home to change into her wetsuit. Soon she was hiking through the sand into the salty foam. She tried to remember everything Skeeter had taught her, but as soon as the first wave swept past her it all came naturally. Paddle out. Turn. Watch for a wave. Feet on the board, left foot first and...

Whoosh!

She took off.

Riley felt a zing of pride as she rode her first wave in. She paddled out again, this time talking a bit with the other kids there. They'd had a good afternoon, though the surf was a little too calm for some of the guys.

It was fine for Riley. As a beginner, she found mellow waves just her speed. As she mounted her board for another wave, Riley thought about Alex and Vance. Vance was cool and fun to hang out with. But she cared about Alex, too. She didn't want to hurt his feelings. And she wanted to be fair to him.

She stood halfway up, then flopped off her board into

the water. Oh, well. Maybe I should focus on the waves instead of thinking about guys all the time, she thought.

She paddled out and waited for another wave.

"Riley!" someone shouted. "Riley..."

She gazed toward the beach. Someone splashed into the surf and paddled toward her on a surfboard. Vance.

She sat up on her board.

[Riley: Okay, I know I promised to avoid him. And it's a big, big ocean. But there's really no escape when you're floating on a board and someone is headed right toward you. I mean, what am I supposed to do? Paddle off to Hawaii?]

"Hi," Riley told him. "The surf is great. Not too rough."

"And the water looks so blue today," he said. "I just grabbed my board and booked out here."

A wave rose up behind Riley. "Here comes one!" she called. She was glad Vance was there—surfing was even more fun when he was around.

She mounted her board and threw her arms out for balance....

And she was riding another wave!

She and Vance surfed until they were exhausted, although Vance had done more stunt falls than anything.

Riley dragged her board up onto the hot sand of the beach.

Vance dropped his board beside hers and sat on it. "Another great day!"

"Really!" Riley sat on her board. "I totally love surfing. It's so much fun!"

"But it really zaps the energy," Vance said, stretching out on his board. "Wake me up when it's time for school."

"Oh, come on, Mr. Rock-Climbing, Triathalon Snowboarder!" Riley teased. "*You're* tired?"

"Hey, even pro athletes need naps," Vance said.

Riley stretched out beside him, loving the smell of the salt water and the feel of the late-afternoon sun on her skin. She knew it was about time to head home for dinner, but she couldn't leave yet. When she was out on the beach, her troubles seemed so small.

"The ocean is amazing," she said. "When my parents first split up, I used to hit the beach a lot. There's a lifeguard stand by my house, and I would sit there after hours. Try to work things out. Argue sides in my head."

"Really?" Vance asked. "And who won?"

"That's the great part about arguing with yourself. You always win."

Vance laughed. "I sort of do the same thing. When I've got something on my mind, I jump on my bike or take off running. Sometimes when things slam you, you just have to kick it and let loose."

Riley sighed. What was she supposed to be worrying about?

Oh, right...Alex and Vance. Somehow it didn't seem so important when she was in the water, floating, waiting for the next wave. Or lying on her board, relaxing in the sand.

She felt a light tug on her hair then looked up.

"I thought I saw a strand of seaweed," Vance said. "Or was that your hair? Salt water is a killer."

Riley laughed. "Oh, right. You'd better rush home and give your hair a moisturizing masque."

"Hey, I do it every night," Vance joked, shaking out his spiky hair.

Riley sighed. She didn't want the day or the afternoon or this moment on the beach to end. She wished she could stay right there forever.

chapter twelve

"So you had a great time surfing with Vance?" Chloe asked Riley in the kitchen that evening.

"Well, yeah," Riley admitted. "Though I totally failed at avoiding him."

"It's no wonder," Chloe said. "You can't run from your soul mate!"

"Vance is not my soul mate," Riley said.

"He is, too!" Chloe didn't understand why her sister kept denying the truth. "The Love Factor doesn't lie, and today was proof."

Riley shook her head. "It's just a quiz, Chloe. I'm not going to believe it."

Frustrated, Chloe looked around the kitchen. "Okay, I'll prove it to you. Manuelo? Can you come here a second? I want to ask you a few questions. . . ."

Five minutes later Chloe wanted to shriek as her purple pen ran down the page of Manuelo's answers. She had asked Manuelo to think of one of his true loves and fill out the quiz. But she had never expected such fabulous results!

"How did I do?" Manuelo asked.

"This is the most perfect score you could possibly get!" Chloe said, looking up from the Love Factor quiz spread out on the kitchen table. This would prove, once and for all, that the quiz worked.

"You're kidding," Riley said, pushing her algebra book aside to take a look. "Manuelo, how did you do this?"

Chloe gaped at him. "The real question is, who is your secret love? I mean, according to this you should run to the nearest courthouse and seal the deal with your soul mate forever."

"Aha," Manuelo said, nodding. He pursed his lips, trying to restrain himself. "That could be a problem."

"What?" Chloe asked. "What's so funny?"

Manuelo dissolved into giggles. "Last time I checked, you could not wed a crustacean. My 'secret love' is not marriage material. When I filled out the quiz , I had but one thing in mind. The love of my palate. Lobster!"

"What?" Chloe sank down in her chair. "A lobster? You can't have a love affair with a lobster!"

"Right. How does that work, Manuelo?" Riley asked.

"It's so simple," Manuelo said, gesturing with a spatula. "Don't you see? To have a relationship with a lobster, there is so little conflict. It never gives me silly gifts. I never get sick of it. And, yes, I did learn my love was not perfect. All that cholesterol! But these small things I can forgive. For that smooth, succulent flesh. The buttery afterglow—"

"Okay!" Riley interrupted him. "I think I've heard enough!"

"Me, too," Chloe said as Manuelo returned to the stove to stir a pot. She was disappointed that the quiz wasn't all it was cracked up to be.

Chloe looked across the table at her sister. "You were right all along. This quiz isn't foolproof. At least, it's not as accurate as I thought."

Riley nodded. "There's no wisdom in the Love Factor," she said.

"I'm sorry I sort of forced it on you," Chloe said.

"That's okay," Riley said. "It made me realize something. I don't really want a boyfriend right now. I just kind of want to go with the flow. Do what I want and not worry about it."

"But that means—" Chloe began.

"I know," Riley finished. "I've got to do something about Alex."

I've got to get out of this date with Dylan, Chloe thought the next morning. But how? She leaned against a brick wall outside the school, wondering how *Teen Style* would handle this.

[<u>Chloe</u>: A. Tell him you're not feeling well. (But then I can't show up at Mango's. And I can't bear to miss the fun, especially if Lennon shows up!)

B. Spill the truth. The note was intended for someone else. He's a great guy, just not your crush. (Ouch! That would be hard to do. I'm not used to being so blunt.) C. Find a friend for him and tell him it was all about a blind date! (Like that's going to happen. I'm having enough trouble getting my own date for Friday night!)]

There's got to be a better way, Chloe thought as Lennon came up the path toward school.

"Hey," he said. "Did you hear about bio class?"

Chloe shook her head.

"We're meeting in the library today," Lennon told her. "Some loser stuck a sea anemone in the air vent, and the lab totally reeks. They've got to air it out before we can go back."

"Gross!" Chloe winced. "Who would do something so stupid?"

Lennon shrugged. "No clue. I don't know everything. Though I can be a know-it-all sometimes."

Chloe felt a wave of embarrassment as she sank against the wall. "So you heard that?"

He nodded. One corner of his mouth lifted, almost in a grin.

"I'm sorry, Lennon. But you do act like the authority on everything."

"And that bothers you?" he asked. "Or does it kill you because I'm usually right?"

Chloe couldn't help but laugh. "You know, Mr. Know-it-all, now that you're here, let's put this to rest. About tomorrow. Are—"

The morning bell rang, right in their ears.

Chloe stared up at it, furious. This was just too much! She wasn't going to fight it anymore.

Lennon made a show of rubbing his ears. "What? What were you saying?" he asked as the bell finally stopped.

"Oh, never mind!" Chloe said, heading for the stairs. It was not meant to be. Fate was keeping her from dating Lennon. And the sooner she accepted that, the better off she would be.

She trudged up the outdoor stairs to the annex. The corridor that lined the second story of the building was already crowded with students on their way to class. Weaving through a group, Chloe spotted Riley walking slowly just ahead of her.

"Riley!" she called, catching up with her. "It just happened again," she said. "I asked Lennon about Friday night, and the bell rang right in our ears."

"Oh, no!" Riley touched her sister's arm. "This is getting bizarre."

"I'm giving up," Chloe said.

"You can't!" Riley insisted. "You really like Lennon."

"But things don't always work out just because you like a guy," Chloe said.

"That's for sure." Riley looked down at her feet.

"Riley!" someone called. It was Alex, hanging with Sierra and Saul at the end of the corridor. "Over here!"

Chloe glanced at him, then back at her sister. "Alex is calling you." Just then, Chloe saw Vance pop up from the stairs at the opposite end of the outdoor platform.

"Hey, Riley!" he shouted.

Riley spun around.

"Got a minute?" Vance asked.

Riley was stuck in the middle, glancing from one boy to the other. "Come on!" she said, grabbing Chloe by the arm. "Time for the artful dodge." She pulled Chloe through the nearest restroom door.

"Oh, Riley," Chloe said sympathetically. "You have to face them sometime—"

Just then a boy pushed past them. Chloe turned around and saw the backs of a few other boys lined up to...

"Ohmigosh!" she exclaimed, pushing Riley back out the door. "Wrong room!"

"The *boys'* room!" Riley clapped her hands to her face. "I've been thinking so hard, I must be suffering from brain drain!"

Chloe found the door to the girls' room next door. "Girls," she said, double-checking the sign before she and Riley ducked inside. They squeezed past a line of girls and went over to the row of gleaming white sinks.

"Phew!" Riley said. "That was close."

"I think you'd better make a decision here," Chloe said. "Before we run out of doors!"

Riley grabbed a paper towel and ran some cold water on it. What should she do? she wondered, pressing it against her neck. "I wish there was an easy way," she told Chloe.

Chloe gave her a look of sympathy. "It's not as simple as the Love Factor quiz makes it sound," she said. "But you've got to do something. You're on a collision course with two guys out there."

Riley nodded. Chloe was right. All this worrying was taking up too much space in her brain. And it wasn't fair to Vance or Alex.

She had to set things straight. Right now.

"Wish me luck," she said, heading toward the door. "I have a feeling I'm going to need it."

chapter thirteen

"Do you want a snack?" Alex asked after school that day. "I can get some chips or iced tea or something."

"No, thanks," Riley said, sinking into the worn couch in his basement. There was a knot of tension in her throat. She knew what she had to say, but it was hard.

His fingers moved over the guitar strings, picking out a familiar melody. It was the song he'd written for Riley.

"Make me want to change...Make me want to speak....Tell you how I feel...You're the one I seek."

Tears stung her eyes, and she lifted a hand to swipe them away.

But Alex noticed. He stopped singing. "Wow. I didn't think I was that far off-key."

"No," Riley said. "It's not the song. It's me."

He watched her, waiting to hear what she had to say to him.

She couldn't say it. She liked him so much. She didn't want to hurt him.

But she had to be honest.

Just say it, Riley. Say it! she told herself.

She swallowed hard and pressed her hands into tight fists. "I can't be your girlfriend anymore," Riley blurted out.

"Wow." Alex stopped strumming and rested his hand atop the guitar. "Why not?"

"Alex, I really, really like you," Riley said. "But I like hanging out with other guys, too. And there's so many different things I want to try, like surfing and *Teen Jeopardy*, and a million other things. I don't want to hurt you—"

"Is this about that Love Factor quiz?" Alex interrupted.

Riley stared at him. "What?"

"My sister has been talking about it all week. This dumb love quiz. She made me take it."

Riley tried not to laugh. "*You* took the quiz? About me?"

Alex nodded. "Yeah, and my sister said we didn't get a very good score. But I don't believe in those things. Do you?"

Riley shook her head. "No. And this isn't about the quiz. I just think we need to be free to hang out with other people. Both of us."

Alex took a deep breath. "Yeah, you have a point. You know, I was thinking the same thing myself."

"Really?" Riley tried to look into his eyes, but Alex was leaning over his guitar now, head down.

Suddenly Alex strummed his guitar. "I *know a girl, her name is* Riley," he sang. "*To make her stop crying,* I'*d walk a mile-y*. . . ."

Riley laughed through her tears. Leave it to Alex to make *her* feel better when *she* was breaking up with *him*. Well…sort of.

"Are we okay?" she asked him. "You don't hate me?"

He shook his head. "I'm going to miss being your boyfriend."

"We'll still be friends," Riley said.

He nodded. "And who knows? Down the road, we could hook up again, right? If we feel like it. I mean, we're only in ninth grade. Anything can happen."

"Anything can happen," Riley said, liking the sound of that. She squeezed his hand. She was so relieved! Everything was turning out okay.

Anything can happen, she thought. And that was how she needed to take things right now—with an open mind and a wide-open date book.

chapter fourteen

On Friday afternoon Riley floated in the lineup with a half-dozen other surfers. She had met Vance on the beach after school, and together they tried to catch some waves.

She'd been surfing for more than an hour, and this was going to be her last wave. She had places to go.

"Heads up," someone called as a wave swelled behind them.

"See if you can ride this one all the way in," Vance said. "I dare you."

"Oh, right!" Riley teased. "You're the one who was just eating sand."

"I meant to do that," Vance said with a huge grin. "I was trying to do a handstand on the board!" His last words were drowned out as the surfers rose onto their boards.

Riley heard the familiar whoosh of water as the

wave kicked up around her, pressing her forward. She held her hands out, working to balance herself. This would have to be her last wave of the day. She wanted to make it count!

She managed to ride it in until it turned to foam.

"Nice one," Vance said from where he'd landed a few feet away. He turned his board and took a wave sideways. "Let's grab another one!"

"I can't," Riley said. "I have to go."

"No way!" Vance insisted.

"I've got plans," Riley said. She had to get showered and dressed for The Wave's show at Mango's. Maybe she wasn't Alex's girlfriend anymore, but she wanted to see Alex and Sierra perform. She had promised to be there to cheer them on.

"Okay," Vance said. "Well, maybe we'll hook up this weekend."

"Maybe," Riley called back to him. "I'll definitely be spending some time here on the beach."

"Later!" Vance shouted as he headed back into the water.

She wrung the water from her hair and carried her board across the sand. So far things were totally casual between her and Vance. Chance meetings. Easygoing jokes. And she liked it that way.

They'd never even kissed.

Something to look forward to, she thought as she trudged up the beach.

• • •

"Where's Riley?" Quinn asked. She sat across the table from Chloe at Mango's.

"Don't worry. She'll be here," Chloe said, scooping some whipped cream off her decaf coffee drink. Beside her, Dylan stirred his fifth packet of sugar into his iced tea. He had insisted on buying drinks for all the girls—Chloe, Quinn, Tara, and Amanda. It was very sweet of him, but Chloe didn't want him to be quite so nice. After all, this was probably going to be their one and only date.

"I can't wait to see The Wave perform," Amanda said. "This is so exciting."

"I'll bet Riley is thrilled," Tara added. "I mean, her boyfriend is the lead guitarist in a rock band!"

Chloe didn't reply. Alex wasn't Riley's boyfriend anymore. But Riley had asked Chloe not to say anything to anyone, at least until the gig was over. Riley didn't want the gossip to overshadow the band.

"I think Alex is a little hurt," Riley had told Chloe when she came home that day. "But he's not mad. It was hard, but now that it's over I feel so much better."

Chloe knew it was for the best. Now she sat at Mango's with her friends, biting her tongue, struggling not to tell them the news. She loved to be the first to break a juicy bit of gossip. But she'd never let Riley down that way.

"Is Sierra nervous?" Quinn asked. "I don't know how

she does it. I would be so freaked getting onstage in front of all my friends."

"I don't think it fazes her," Chloe said. "I guess her parents started her early with those violin recitals."

"Do you know what this place used to be?" Dylan asked. When the girls shook their heads, he answered, "A video parlor! I used to come here all the time. Then California cuisine hit, and the owner turned it into this fruity, organic teen club."

"Really?" Chloe said politely. "I didn't know that. Are you into video games, Dylan?"

He smiled, a silver flash of braces. "I'm pretty much an expert. I know most of the tricks to get to the top level. Now I mostly do computer games."

Chloe smiled back, trying to appear impressed. Dylan wasn't a bad guy...just not her kind of guy. There was definitely no Love Factor with him.

"They've got some decent games here," Dylan said. He looked longingly at one of the PCs where his friends were gathered. "Do you want to see?"

Chloe could tell he was dying to get away. What? He'd rather be playing games with his friends than on this *sensational* date with her?

Chloe laughed to herself. I guess the Love Factor thing works both ways, she thought. I don't have "the factor" for him any more than he has it for me.

"I can show you a few shortcuts in the games," Dylan said.

"Maybe later," Chloe said. "But why don't you go check it out, Dylan? We'll be right here, saving the table for when the band starts."

Dylan took a swig of tea, then swiped at his mouth. "Okay. I'll catch you later."

"He's sweet," Tara said.

Chloe nodded sadly. "But he's not Lennon. I guess I really messed up."

"It's not your fault," Quinn insisted. "Besides, your friends are here to save the night. We're going to have a blast—no matter what boys show up."

"Thanks, guys," Chloe said. She was glad Tara and Quinn had agreed to stick with her. If you've got your friends, nothing else matters.

Riley breezed in, the back of her hair still wet. She scanned the crowd, searching for her sister.

Chloe waved to her. "Over here!"

Riley plunked herself down in an empty chair. "I didn't miss anything, did I?"

"They're just about to start," Chloe said. "Alex and Saul have been testing the sound system."

A few minutes later the band members took their places. Alex leaned into the mike. "Hey, everybody," he said. "We're The Wave. Now let's rock!"

Saul counted off on the drums—"One, two, three, four!"—and the group launched into a song.

As Alex sang, Chloe saw the look he shot at Riley. Wow! He still liked her! At least, it seemed that way to Chloe.

But Riley had made her choice.

Someone tapped her shoulder. Chloe turned, and her heart started beating like crazy. "Lennon?"

> **[Chloe: He's here! He showed. Happy dance in my heart! I would do it on the dance floor, but that would look stupid with the song the band is playing.]**

He stood behind her, grinning. "Hey. Mind if a know-it-all sits at your table?"

Chloe let out a breath. "I'm glad you came." She couldn't take her eyes off him as he sat down beside her. Was he here by coincidence, or did he really get the message about their date?

"Hey, I wouldn't miss our date," he said. He glanced over at Dylan, who was heavy into a game at a computer. "Even if you are double-booked."

"That note was meant for you," Chloe said. "But you knew? You knew what I was trying to ask you all along?"

"Only because one of my friends heard about it from your friend Tara," he said. "What, were you afraid to ask me? Why couldn't you spit it out?"

Chloe sighed. "If only you knew!" she cried. "I guess I'm not the best communicator in the world."

Lennon moved closer. "You—"

Just then the band launched into a loud rock song, overpowering his voice.

"What?" Chloe yelled above the music, dying to

know what he had to say. But she couldn't hear a thing.

Lennon smiled and leaned very close, until his lips were touching hers in a soft kiss.

Breathless, Chloe closed her eyes and kissed him back. Now *that* message was perfectly clear!

mary-kate olsen ashley olsen

so little time

Chloe and Riley's

SCRAPBOOK

My sister, Chloe, is on a mission. A mission to date her perfect match.

Hey, funny bumping into you here.
But we're standing in front of my locker!

I'll bet you ten bucks I have him by the end of the week.
You're on!

So, what will it be? Coffee, tea...
A date?

So much to do! So little time!

I wonder if Chloe is free on Saturday.

Here's a sneak peek at

so little time

Book 9
dating game

Suddenly, Riley experienced a feeling of dread. If Mom and Dad decided not to go to the Save the Seals dance, then she and Chloe would not be attending either. And it was always so much fun. Plus, it was tradition for Mom and Dad to burn up the dance floor at the event during the disco songs.

Jake grabbed a protein bar from the pantry and shrugged his shoulders. "Let's just go together. We'll chaperone the girls. What's the big deal?"

"It *is* a big deal," Mom argued.

Chloe turned to Riley with a worried look.

"If we're separated," Macy went on, "then it's in the best interest of all concerned that we remain...*separate*."

Riley leaned in to whisper to Chloe. "I've got an idea. We should help them find dates for the dance."

"Before or after we find our *own* dates?" Chloe said back. "So far, nobody is picking *us* up on Saturday night."

Riley nodded in miserable agreement.

"But you may have a point," Chloe murmured under her breath. "Because if we don't find *them* dates, there will be no reason to find ourselves dates."

"I know," Riley said. "So, how should we—"

"We have the perfect solution," Chloe said out loud. Her voice rang with a great air of confidence.

Mom and Dad looked at them with interest.

"We'll find you dates for Saturday night," Chloe said.

"Uh...yeah," Riley stammered even though she wasn't quite ready for Chloe to blurt out this idea. They didn't have a plan yet.

Dad beamed at Mom then nodded thankfully to them. "I think I'll take you up on that. Make sure she's smart and beautiful." He laughed a little.

But Mom didn't look so thrilled about the idea. She cleared her throat. "I don't need my children to help me get a date. I'll find my own escort, thank you."

Riley breathed a sigh of relief. Their chance to go to the dance was safe—for the moment.

Dad chomped down on the protein bar, grinning as if he didn't have a care in the world. "This is great, girls. I'd better try on my suit and make sure it still fits. See you later!" He headed out of the house.

Mom sighed and started for her office. "Girls, you might want to make a snack. I've got a conference call scheduled with a buyer overseas, so we'll be having dinner a bit later than usual."

Almost instantly, Chloe opened the fridge and

pulled out yogurt, strawberries, pineapple, and skim milk, then reached into the cabinet for the wheat germ.

"What are you doing?" Riley asked.

"Making a smoothie," Chloe said. "Want one?"

Not feeling very hungry, Riley shook her head. "Where are we going to find a smart and beautiful woman for Dad in five days?"

Chloe shrugged. "I don't know, but wouldn't it be great if she came with two smart and cute boys for us?"

Riley giggled, in part because the idea sounded ridiculous, but also because she had to admit, at the same time, it sounded great!

Chloe was channel surfing, listening to the radio, sipping on her smoothie, and talking on the phone with Tara—all at the same time.

"I can't believe that Lennon didn't ask you to Save the Whales," Tara was saying.

"Save the Seals," Chloe corrected her.

"Whatever," Tara chirped. "Whales, seals, baby dolphins—the point is, he *didn't* ask you. And you dropped some serious hints. I mean, you were looking pretty desperate there for a minute."

Desperate? Chloe thought. Was it really that bad?

[Chloe: Okay, here's the best part about moments like this: One day they will be over. Right now it seems so tragic. I mean, it's practically Shakespeare or at the very least, a really

dramatic episode of *Seventh Heaven*. But in some not too distant future, it will barely register as a memorable event. Of course, right now I'm totally freaking out and thinking I might have to move to Iowa to escape the humiliation.]

"Are you there?" Tara asked.

"Yes, I'm here," Chloe grumbled. "I'm trying to factor the social damage. Did everyone see me throw myself at Lennon and be completely ignored?"

"No," Tara said. "It was all pretty low key."

The Call Waiting sounded in Chloe's ear. "Hold on, someone's beeping in." She hit the Flash button on her phone. "Hello?"

"Is this Chloe Carlson?" a female voice asked.

The woman sounded very familiar, but Chloe couldn't quite place her. "Yes, who's this?" she asked.

"It's Ms. Raffin, dear. Listen, I'm so glad that I caught you. The school paper's in a terrible bind, and we need your help."

"But Riley's the one who writes for the paper," Chloe said.

"Oh, I realize that, dear. I couldn't help overhearing you in the hall today discussing your interest in writing a Sound Off."

On that note, Chloe reached for her smoothie and took a generous sip. Ms. Raffin didn't exactly overhear as much as she eavesdropped. Sometimes she knew more about who was starting up, breaking up, and making up at West Malibu High than the students themselves!

"Could you work up something by tomorrow morning?" Ms. Raffin asked.

Chloe paused to allow the smoothie to go down. Suddenly she felt a sharp pain pierce her sinuses, then a horrible ache in her temples. The smoothie had given her a brain freeze!

Chloe opened her mouth to speak, but nothing came out. Waving her free hand like crazy, she prayed it would pass before...

"I'm staring at empty column space where the original Sound Off column should have gone," Ms. Raffin continued. "But no matter how bad the pizza is, I can't dedicate two columns in a row to the subject." The teacher paused. "I don't hear anything. That must be a yes. Very well. See you tomorrow, dear. And thanks a bunch." *Click*.

Chloe sucked in a breath. "Wait!" The brain freeze ended. She could speak now. As if it mattered.

Riley walked into the room. "Dinner's almost ready," she said.

Chloe couldn't imagine sitting down to eat right now. Her mind was racing a million miles a minute.

Riley's gaze zeroed in on the phone in Chloe's hand. "Who are you talking to?"

Suddenly, Chloe remembered Tara on the other line and pressed the Flash button. "Tara, I'll have to call you later."

"Was that Lennon?" Tara asked.

"I wish." Chloe groaned. "I have to go. Bye." She hung up and buried a pillow in her face.

"What's wrong?" Riley asked.

Chloe removed the pillow and brought Riley up to speed on the entire Ms. Raffin incident.

Riley perched herself on the edge of the bed. "This is no big deal. The Sound Offs are short, like, maybe one page."

This news did nothing to calm down Chloe. "But I have no idea what to write about, and she expects it tomorrow morning!"

Riley considered this for a moment. "I remember seeing a famous author on television and her advice for all new writers was to write what you know."

Chloe felt the urge to push Riley off the bed. "That still doesn't tell me what to write!"

Riley gave her sister a shrewd look. "Think about what you know."

Chloe tried to concentrate, then gave up in frustration. "Ugh! I can't even think straight. This whole Lennon thing is driving me nuts. Can you believe him? I mean, when a girl tells a boy that a dance is coming up, then he should take that as a hint to ask her out!"

Riley smiled. "My point exactly. Write about that."

Chloe was stunned. "Seriously?"

"Why not? It's an issue that you feel passionately about. That's what the Sound Off column is there for."

Chloe warmed up to the idea. "You're right!" She stomped over to the desk and snatched her laptop, booting it up as soon as she returned to the bed.

"Don't get started now," Riley said. "We're about to have dinner."

But Chloe was already turning on the word processing program. "Tell Mom I'm not hungry. I'll put something in the microwave later."

"Okay," Riley said.

Chloe barely noticed her sister leave the room. She was too wrapped up in her first Sound Off. And once Lennon read it, he would know exactly what to do.

Hopefully.

SO LITTLE TIME
Secret Crush Prize Pack Sweepstakes

OFFICIAL RULES:

1.No purchase necessary.

2.To enter complete the official entry form or hand print your name, address, age, and phone number along with the words "SO LITTLE TIME Secret Crush Prize Pack Sweepstakes" on a 3" x 5" card and mail to: SO LITTLE TIME Secret Crush Prize Pack Sweepstakes, c/o HarperEntertainment, Attn: Children's Marketing Department, 10 East 53rd Street, New York, NY 10022. Entries must be received no later than April 30, 2003. Enter as often as you wish, but each entry must be mailed separately. One entry per envelope. Partially completed, illegible, or mechanically reproduced entries will not be accepted. Sponsors are not responsible for lost, late, mutilated, illegible, stolen, postage due, incomplete, or misdirected entries. All entries become the property of Dualstar Entertainment Group, LLC, and will not be returned.

3.Sweepstakes open to all legal residents of the United States (excluding Colorado and Rhode Island) who are between the ages of five and fifteen on April 30, 2003, excluding employees and immediate family members of HarperCollins Publishers, Inc. ("HarperCollins"), Parachute Properties and Parachute Press, Inc., and their respective subsidiaries and affiliates, officers, directors, shareholders, employees, agents, attorneys, and other representatives (individually and collectively "Parachute"), Dualstar Entertainment Group, LLC, and its subsidiaries and affiliates, officers, directors, shareholders, employees, agents, attorneys, and other representatives (individually and collectively "Dualstar"), and their respective parent companies, affiliates, subsidiaries, advertising, promotion and fulfillment agencies, and the persons with whom each of the above are domiciled. Offer void where prohibited or restricted by law.

4.Odds of winning depend on the total number of entries received. Approximately 225,000 sweepstakes announcements published. All prizes will be awarded. Winners will be randomly drawn on or about May 15, 2003, by HarperEntertainment, whose decisions are final. Potential winners will be notified by mail and will be required to sign and return an affidavit of eligibility and release of liability within 14 days of notification. Prizes won by minors will be awarded to parent or legal guardian who must sign and return all required legal documents. By acceptance of their prize, winners consent to the use of their names, photographs, likeness, and personal information by HarperCollins, Parachute, Dualstar, and for publicity purposes without further compensation except where prohibited.

5.Twenty (20) Grand Prize Winners will win a Secret Crush Prize Pack which includes the following: a *Crush Course* videogame; a journal; pen; stationery; lip gloss; and an autographed SO LITTLE TIME: SECRET CRUSH book. Sponsor reserves the right to substitute another prize of equal or greater value in the event that the winner is unable to receive the prize for any reason. Approximate retail value per prize: $70.00.

6.Only one prize will be awarded per individual, family, or household. Prizes are non-transferable and cannot be sold or redeemed for cash. No cash substitute is available. Any federal, state, or local taxes are the responsibility of the winner. Sponsor may substitute prize of equal or greater value, if necessary, due to availability.

7.Additional terms: By participating, entrants agree a) to the official rules and decisions of the judges, which will be final in all respects; and to waive any claim to ambiguity of the official rules and b) to release, discharge, and hold harmless HarperCollins, Parachute, Dualstar, and their affiliates, subsidiaries, and advertising and promotion agencies from and against any and all liability or damages associated with acceptance, use, or misuse of any prize received in this sweepstakes.

8. Any dispute arising from this Sweepstakes will be determined according to the laws of the State of New York, without reference to its conflict of law principles, and the entrants consent to the personal jurisdiction of the State and Federal courts located in New York County and agree that such courts have exclusive jurisdiction over all such disputes.

9.To obtain the name of the winners, please send your request and a self-addressed stamped envelope (excluding residents of Vermont and Washington) to SO LITTLE TIME Secret Crush Prize Pack Sweepstakes, c/o HarperEntertainment, Attn: Children's Marketing Department, 10 East 53rd Street, New York, NY 10022 by June 1, 2003. Sweepstakes Sponsor: HarperCollins Publishers, Inc.